Life Is Just A Bowl Of Cherries

A Collection of Stories
with a Twist.....

....Some About Trees.

Compiled & Edited by Tracey Regan

This edition published in 2019 by Tracey Regan.
Readers who are interested are invited to visit our website at www.tregan.biz

(c) The Long Man / The Final Hour / Arboreal - Ross Cameron
(c) Sixth Sense / Snakes and Ladders - Kelly Van Nelson
(c) Echoes of Ella - Teena Raffa-Mulligan
(c) Train Ride to Death - Maggie Taylor
(c) Where Blue and Green Meet - Johanna Baker-Dowdell
(c) Truth Be Told / Evolution / The Final Solution /The Sweetest Gift /
Making Up For Lost Time / Breakdown / The Day After / The Ultimate Seduction / What's In It For
Me? - Tracey Regan

ISBN : 978 0 6487192 0 5

Introduction

What an amazing, wonderful world we live in!

Amazing that anyone can decide to put together a collection of short stories and 'just put it out there'. Being able to self-publish a book, for a relatively small cost, and expose it to a potential market of hundreds of millions, truly is amazing.

Sorry! Amazing is my favourite word right now! But … wow…. I'm so excited to be able to share this collection with you, from some very talented writers. We've also included a couple of screenplays, from Ross Cameron, an ex-film producer, so we'd love to know what you think about reading short stories in that format.

'Putting it out there' is great, but according to Google, there are around 130 million books available in the world! And since we're just starting out with the 'Bowl of Cherries' series, we'll just have to see what happens.

We are working on a collection of stories about divorce and separation and at the other end of the spectrum would love to share a collection of stories that make you laugh out loud. So if you have a story we can include in our next collection, contact me via www. treganbiz/bowlofcherries I'd love to read your story! Stories are at the core of how humans communicate, and I believe we all have a story to tell, so really - don't hesitate to reach out with your story!

Did you know story telling is good for your health! It can actually reduce your blood pressure, so write that story, or even record it if you don't want to write. Jonathan Gottschall says in his book, The Story Telling Animal, that we as a species are so addicted to stories that when our body goes to sleep, our mind wakes up!

Most of these stories will take you less than 10 minutes to read, and I'm hoping that some will leave you thinking.

It would be great to get any feedback, good or bad, so don't hesitate to reach out and let me know what you think.

HAPPY READING!

CONTENTS

Arboreal	Ross Cameron	1
Truth Be Told	Tracey Regan	9
Where Blue and Green Meet	Johanna Baker-Dowdell	13
Evolution	Tracey Regan	27
Except from The Final Solution	Tracey Regan	29
The Sweetest Gift	Tracey Regan	39
Echoes of Ella	Teena Raffa-Mulligan	53
The Final Hour	Ross Cameron	61
Making Up For Lost Time	Tracey Regan	87
Bush Tragedy	Tracey Regan	93
Snakes and Ladders	Kelly Van Nelson	99
The Ultimate Seduction	Tracey Regan	107
What's In It For Me?	Tracey Regan	113
Breakdown	Tracey Regan	119
The Long Man	Ross Cameron	125
Train Ride To Death	Maggie Taylor	175
About The Authors		181
Sixth Sense	Kelly Van Nelson	185

Arboreal

- Ross Cameron

Andrew DeVere Crane first realised he was turning into a tree when he began to think like a Mountain Ash. And why did they call him Rowan anyway?

Thinking back, he supposed it started at Hendon when he was a cadet. It was 'Mr Bean' in those days, but after he had graduated, the actor he resembled appeared as a police superintendent in a comedy series and that was that.

On day one at Hackney 'nick', his first posting, a bright spark named Cooper, with all of six months more experience than him, had tagged him in the muster room; "come on Rowan, you're with me." The name stuck and now, with five years and a promotion to sergeant under his belt, most people thought it was his given.

Only senior management ever used his full name and he had dropped DeVere in everything but official reports; most people called him Rowan except CID who, behind his back, still called him Mr Bean.

"Is that why I feel like a tree," he thought. "Has the constant reference to Rowan made me susceptible to auto-suggestion." He frowned as he studied his milky coffee. "But if that were true why don't I feel like the actor? Why a tree?"

It was a Saturday afternoon and Andrew was sitting at an outside table of the cafe in the middle of Hackney Downs, part of a plain clothes stake-out awaiting a minor drug transaction. 'Matey' was a low level dealer whose main manor was usually Soho but did a 'bit of trade' locally.

On Friday night CID had arrested a 'hooray' outside a club in Hoxton known to be lax on prevention. He was snorting directly from the packet using a silver spoon while waiting in the queue, which included a team sent specifically to lift whoever they could. He'd panicked after a couple of hours in the cells and given up his supplier, one Stanley Tyrel, obviously known as 'Stan the Man'.

Hooray Henry had made a call from the Police station at three in the morning for 'a couple of downloads for Saturday night' and set up a meet at two the following afternoon. The location was Tyrel's choice and, as expected, he was working 'dealer's flexi-time.' It was three o'clock and hooray Henry was fidgeting. Two plain clothes WPCs were watching from inside the cafe, two CID men, one in his fifties, carrying about two stone too much, mostly around his gut, the other younger but smoking a roll-up and not exactly healthy looking, were strolling about nearby and Andrew was on his second coffee. Matey boy had not appeared but nobody was surprised.

At three fifteen a vintage GS pulled up in the service road by the cafe. Mirror chromed side pods, multi wing mirrors and handle tassels announced the driver as somebody living in the past or making a statement. The grey, belted gaberdine macintosh underlined the 'mod' look and he removed his crash helmet as he walked directly to Henry, who rose to greet him with an outstretched hand.

The mod was a slim but tough looking guy with a fighter's face, broken nose, thickening around the cheek bones and well battered ears. His hand went first to a mac pocket then, as they shook hands, Andrew saw the exchange. Tyrel concealed the stash well but Henry was more clumsy; folded twenties easily visible. Henry gushed, 'How you been Stan, you up for a coffee?' but he couldn't stop himself looking at Crane for approval.

Tyrel frowned and looked around, noting the two girls and the CID men, one of whom had moved between him and the scooter. He dropped his helmet, turned, grabbed Henry's lapels and head butted him hard before taking off at a run directly away from the detectives. Henry screamed and blood gushed from his nose; the girls got tangled in their chairs and the man nearest Tyrel, the fat one, started to run but gave up after twenty yards. The other CID man kept after Tyrel, who was heading for the Pembury estate with a big lead and didn't look like getting caught.

Andrew stood up when the drug dealer nutted Henry but remained rooted to the spot. He was never going to catch Tyrel and reckoned once the fugitive was in the Pembury he would disappear fast, so he reviewed the operation and his options. A sparrow landed on his shoulder, or did he imagine that.

Later, there had been a review, it sounded grand when the 'super' referred to 'a debrief' but it was basically a blame session. Tyrel wasn't a big player but he might have led higher if they had got him in the nick and alerted the drug squad. As it was, he was long gone and the scooter turned out to have been reported stolen the previous week. Nobody had a record of where he lived and 'Henry', who had his nose in a splint and could hardly speak, was refusing to cooperate further.

"Are we keeping you from something Sergeant Crane?" snapped Chief Superintendent Alfred (don't call me Alf) Fisher.

Andrew took his eyes off the small square of sky he was

contemplating through the 'super's' office window and looked at Fisher quizzically. "No Sir" he replied. "But I rather think we might be better employed looking into the stolen scooter and alerting West End to keep their eyes open for Tyrel, than standing here recriminating."

Fisher glared at his sergeant and narrowed his eyes. "Get back to work you lot" he said through gritted teeth. "Except you DeVere Crane, you stay if you please." The hapless bunch slunk out and when the door closed Fisher sat down, slowly shaking his head. Andrew knew what was coming and wondered why he should put up with it. Was he really cut out to be a policeman? Had he ever really felt part of a unit?

He had been a solitary but not lonely child, happy in his own company but keen to mix when the opportunity arose. For the first part of his life he and his mother lived with granddad just outside a small village in rural Essex. He didn't remember his father but Granddad Sam had taken some of the responsibility his son rejected and had loved the boy unconditionally.

Sam Crane was a man of principal and had given Lucy DeVere a home when her parents disowned her for getting pregnant by a farm hand's son, "one of our workers for Heaven's sake." Lucy moved in with the Cranes, father and son, when she was thirty weeks and Fred Crane left when Andrew was two years old. Fred left Lucy distraught and his father ashamed.

Sam died when Andrew was seven and Lucy had to get out of the tied cottage. She had swallowed her pride and begged her father to repent but he was a dyed-in-the-wool bigot and treated her as if she were what she appeared; the daughter of a labourer who should think herself lucky she had lived without paying rent while her old gaffer could still be useful. Her mother would have interceded but she had died a few years earlier leaving her husband even more of an arse wipe.

He gave her short shift so she consolidated what little value Sam owned and moved to London. An old friend gave her a room in a large Victorian house just off 'Vicky' Park in Hackney and life started getting better almost immediately.

The friend, Fiona Warhurst, had been married to an advertising executive who couldn't keep it in his pants and after the divorce she copped the house and a good regular allowance to bring up the two children. To keep busy she started a florist shop at the 'good end' of Cambridge Heath Road and needed somebody to look after it.

Fiona enjoyed setting up the shop and buying stock early mornings in New Covent Garden but got easily bored maning the business all day. Lucy got paid well and loved it. Life rapidly improved.

After initial reticence on all sides, Andrew became friends with Fiona's children, a girl of his age and a younger boy. He was accepted into Lauristan Road School where he kept mostly to himself then progressed to Upton House Secondary. He didn't excel but generally enjoyed himself, did some serious running in his teens and left after the fifth year with enough GCEs to be accepted into the Police Academy at Hendon. He met Shirley, who was to become his wife, in a youth club at Hackney Wick during his last year at Upton House.

For some reason, as he left Alf Fisher's office, Andrew was thinking about his school days. Fisher reminded him of his old head master Tom Morrish, a well-intentioned buffoon who seemed to stroll around issuing platitudes to all and sundry while the deputy head, Richard Payne, ran the school.

Andrew realised now that Morrish must have done more than was obvious but Payne was feared, loathed and respected in equal measure and appeared to the boys to run the school. He taught Maths and was good at it. Andrew got his 'O' levels which he hadn't expected and looking back he had the feeling Payne's demeanour had actually helped him achieve. A rare visit to Morrish's office for a dressing down was more a 'you've let the school down, you've let your teacher down and on and on and on'. Fisher's bollocking was very similar and achieved DeVere Crane to thinking whether he should leave the force and concentrate on his metamorphosis.

In the evening, as he started his walk home through St John's churchyard, heading for his semi-detached in Morning Lane after completing his required hours to qualify for overtime, Andrew was thinking how nice it would be to soak his feet. At the boundary of the churchyard was a newish park where a small fountain commemorated something or other and he stopped there. Without really thinking much about it he removed his shoes and socks and stood in the water. It was only a few inches deep and pleasantly warm and the effect was immediate.

He stopped reviewing the afternoon's fuck up, he stopped worrying about Fisher or thinking of school days; he stopped thinking. Life went on around him and he was aware of the sounds of a Saturday night, of people staring, some teenagers laughing, the church bell tolling nine o'clock; the stars singing.

He let go of inhibition and spread his arms wide. He felt more alive than he ever had as he breathed out his Carbon Dioxide rather than breathing in the Oxygen and his back stiffened. He felt powerful but passive. He felt green.

Truth Be Told
- Tracey Regan

The day it happened changed his life forever. Not that anyone else would notice. But still, change his life it did and now he had to live with a secret that he could never tell. For many years he had enjoyed the grey, cold mornings of winter and the bright summer days he had spent in the wood on top of the lonely hill on the farm property of Simon and Sarah Watson. They would race their horses up to the top of the hill and he would watch with envy, as every day they would rest and have a drink under the shade of the tallest tree, exhausted and breathless.

In the early days, they had been so happy. Laughing and playful, they would kiss for what seemed like hours, and sometimes make love in the sunshine and carve their names in the bark of a tree. But over the years, those lingering moments seemed to get less and less. Where there was once laughter, now there were stony glances and harsh words. More often these days, they came alone and did not stay for long.

The day it happened was crisp and cool. The first hint of winter left an icy feel to the grass, and a lazy, lingering curl of smoke could be seen rising from the farmhouse, as the dawn lit up the clear blue sky. The ground around him began to shake, as he recognised both Simon and Sarah begin their morning ride to exercise the horses. He loved the way the ground beat like a drum, stronger, faster and louder as they approached the top of the hill. He smiled to himself, hoping today they would share some kind words.

Sarah reached the top first, her breath coming hard and fast as she tied her frisky horse to the branch of the tree. He had never seen this horse before and it snorted and stamped angrily as Simon caught up.

"… I told you not to ride that damn horse…," Simon sneered as he took a swig from his hip flask, "you might hurt yourself riding a horse like that you know." The thought made him laugh out loud.

"Second thoughts, keep riding it," his laughing became uncontrollable.

"Oh for God's sake Simon, it's barely dawn and you're drinking already."

"….still drinking … not been to bed …" Simon sucked hard on the bottle.

"And what would you know about it anyway? Everything you know about horses you learnt from me." There was a look of such disgust on Sarah's face and Simon could not contain his rage.

"When are we going to put an end to all this shit?"

"We've been through this a million times Simon and every different scenario. But as you well know, it comes down to this. We can live separately in the same house, but my frigging uncle left an iron-clad will. If we get divorced or separated, you get nothing, and I get to live on an allowance of 30 grand a year. I am NOT gonna let that happen…."

"Same old story sweetie," said Simon taking another long swig on his flask. " I'm just saying no matter what the deal, I don't think I can take it anymore. I think it's time to take action and maybe that time is now."

Simon shakily pulled a small, shiny revolver from his pocket. Sarah laughed, a long slow laugh, almost a snort, just like the stallion still snorting and stomping next to them.

"…and what exactly are you going to do with that? You really want to shoot me? You're an idiot. I don't think you've thought this through. You'll just end up broke and in prison…."

"JUST STOP TALKING!" He watched, as Simon drunkenly rushed toward Sarah. He wanted to do something, anything to stop him from hurting her, but could not move. He shouted loudly to the wind, but could not be heard.

Simon fired a shot, which didn't seem to hit any target, and he staggered and reeled wildly as he fell to the ground. The rock that hit Simon's head as he fell had no say in the matter. The jagged edge went sharply into his temple, and Simon's body slumped into lifelessness. Sarah began to scream, loudly at first, so loud that the birds nesting in the branches above scattered quickly. Over time, the screams became gasps, as she gulped in large bowlfuls of air.

Sarah stared at the ground for what he felt was an eternity, just thinking. Suddenly she grabbed her horse, still stomping and snorting, and hooked Simon's boot into the stirrup of the saddle. With a huge slap on his rump, she sent him galloping down the hillside towards the farm, out of control and dragging Simon's limp body behind it. She quickly searched around for the revolver and threw it into the dam behind the hill. He thought he saw the faint hint of a smile on Sarah's lips.

They both stood for a while staring blankly, and for a very short moment he thought she had glanced at him. He shivered and wondered if he would ever see her on the hilltop again. He understood her reasoning of course, but it didn't make him feel good about it. No-one would doubt Sarah's explanation, the horse was out of control after.all. But he knew what had happened. He had seen it all, and could tell no-one.

Where Blue and Green Meet
- Johanna Baker-Dowdell

Sarah held the delicate winged seed in her hands, gently cupping it so as not to lose her precious cargo. She had bent down to pick it up a moment earlier, rolling the soft paper-like casing that surrounded the flat seed between her fingertips. The sensation comforted Sarah and this ritual was one she repeated daily as the seeds fell in late spring.

The seeds had started falling in flurries a few days before as an unseasonably strong Hebridean wind whipped around the southern tip of Sleat peninsula. Winds were not uncommon at the farm, which was located just south of Armadale on the Isle of Skye, but they tended to be much more gentle during spring. As a result the papery seeds now covered the ground in a haphazard ring around the elm tree. Sarah approached the tree and felt a gentle crunch under her feet as she ran her fingers along the rough, sturdy trunk of the elm before sitting down against it. This was Sarah McKinnon's favourite place to think; a place she had been visiting when she needed to be alone ever since she was a child. Sarah brushed the tips of her fingers lightly across the scattered seeds and allowed her thoughts to drift back almost 20 years to when she had smuggled three identical seeds out of Tasmania. The girl she had been had carefully wrapped the fragile seeds in her grandmother's monogrammed handkerchief and then concealed the package deep in her pocket. Although both her older sisters lived in Australia, Sarah had only visited the faraway country once. That trip held bittersweet memories for her - still. Sarah indulged herself, allowing her memories to crowd her mind and push the nagging thoughts of household commitments out.

~~~
~~~

"Sarah have you finished packing yet?" Hope asked in the exasperated tone she usually adopted when speaking with her younger sister. "We'll miss the ferry if you don't hurry. And I don't need to stay on this boring old island a second longer than necessary!" She added a sigh for good measure.

Hope and her twin sister Grace were 21 and impatient to do something with their lives. They had been planning a trip to Australia for years and were still livid their parents had made them wait until Sarah finished school so she could go with them. Both were sure Sarah would cramp their style and had been hatching a plan to dump her as soon as possible after arriving in the Antipodes.

"Stop hassling me!" Sarah retorted, throwing Hope a withering look. "I was just weighing my suitcase to make sure it was still within my limit after I added some extra books."

"You and your books! If you spent less time with your nose stuck in between those pages and more time talking to real people you might actually have a social life," Hope said scornfully.

"I have a social life, thank you very much! My friends even threw me a going away party last night."

"I don't think your latest book group meeting could be categorised as a party, but if those silly bookworms are going to miss you so much why don't you stay here?" Hope's right eyebrow arched as she said the words. "We wouldn't want to deny them your company."

"Stop being such a cow Hope. Anyway, I'm not missing this trip for anything; I know my life is going to change in Australia and I'm not letting you or Grace get in the way of that happening."

"So be it Sarah, but let this be a warning to you: if your

imagination gets us into trouble, Grace and I will have no issue with leaving you behind."

Hope's steely stare confirmed she meant every one of those words and Sarah shivered involuntarily. Surely her sisters wouldn't leave her alone on the other side of the world, would they?

Before she had time to contemplate what that would mean, Sarah's father had bundled her into their green metallic station wagon and called impatiently to her sisters to hurry up. It was only a short drive from their Armadale home to the dock where the ferry travelled from the Isle of Skye to Mallaig on the mainland. While each girl was able to carry her own suitcase and handbag, their parents wanted to see the three girls off on their grand antipodean adventure.

Fellow travellers were already boarding the ferry when the McKinnon's car spluttered to a stop at the dockside. Hurried hugs and kisses followed and the excited trio ran for the boat, determined not to miss their ticket off what they all considered to be a stuffy island. Sarah saw her parents move close to hold each other tightly and felt a lump form in her throat. She fought back tears as she waved goodbye to them and the ferry slowly moved further and further away from the place she called home.

By the time the McKinnon sisters arrived at Heathrow the following day, their nervous excitement and exhaustion had them bickering and squabbling. Even the twins, who usually finished each other's sentences, were now alternating between reading excerpts from the Australian guidebook to each other and fighting over where they would stay in Sydney on the night they all arrived in this far-flung country. Sarah didn't care; she just hunched herself into a slightly smaller shape in the plastic airport chair and lowered her gaze to her favourite escape, Shakespeare's A Midsummer's Night's Dream. This play had enchanted the 13-year-old Sarah when she had studied it in English and the well-thumbed text hadn't left her presence in the five years since. The play was to Sarah what the rabbit hole was to Alice.

~~~

Four weeks later the sisters arrived in Launceston, well tanned and travel-worn after making their way down Australia's east coast from Sydney to Melbourne and then catching another ferry to the island where their spinster aunt Mary - their mother's older sister - now lived. Her Scottish accent was still noticeable after 10 years away from Skye, but her nieces could faintly hear how the Australian accent had roughened the edges on some of her words, and how her speech had slowed ever so slightly.

Mary was pretty straight-laced and took her duties as guardian to her three young nieces very seriously, so the girls were surprised when she suggested they attend a music festival at The Basin in Cataract Gorge the following night. Mary's neat blue cottage with white doors, windows and iron lacework was only a few hundred metres from the gorge so the girls decided to explore the scene of this exciting event while their aunt napped that afternoon.

Hope and Grace ran ahead of Sarah, holding each other's hands tightly and giggling uncontrollably as they ran down the hill towards the lush green haven ahead. Sarah knew they resented her tagging along with them, but the past month had been so eye opening and thrilling for all three that they had started to grow closer.

As she stepped through the wrought iron gates that signalled the entrance to Cataract Gorge, Sarah caught a flash of green and blue out of the corner of her eye. She quickly swung around to see a
~~~

stunning peacock stalking haughtily through the undergrowth. Sarah had never seen a real peacock before (she didn't count the 20 or so dusty feathers her mother proudly displayed in a vase in their dining room) and stood like a statue for a few seconds before realising she should be taking a photo. She fumbled in her handbag for a few more seconds and pulled on the camera strap, tipping out most of the bag's contents on to the ground in the same motion. By the time she looked up again, the mysterious creature had disappeared.

Sarah hurriedly packed everything back into her bag and ran down the hill to catch up with her sisters, who were sitting on the grass in the shade of an elm tree. As she looked at the tree's towering limbs and expansive canopy Sarah was reminded of her favourite quote from Titania, Queen of the Fairies, in A Midsummer's Night's Dream.

"So doth the woodbine the sweet honeysuckle gently entwist. The female ivy so enrings the barky fingers of the elm. Oh, how I love thee! How I dote on thee!" Sarah recited, a secretive smile forming at the corners of her mouth.

"What are you mumbling crazy Sarah?" Grace exclaimed, rolling her eyes. Sarah's smile quickly turned to embarrassment, which she covered up by asking, "Did you see the peacock?"

"No, where was it?" Grace asked, turning her head to look behind the tree.

"I think she imagined it," Hope giggled.

"I did not! I tried to take a photo but it disappeared into the bushes before I had the chance. I'm sure we'll see it on the way back," Sarah said, looking Hope squarely in the eye.

"Oh, who cares," Hope said dismissively as she stood up.

"We've got some exploring to do so we know where to sit tomorrow night."

"Don't you mean we need to find out where the boys sit," Grace quipped, and the twins giggled conspiratorially together.

As Grace stood up from where they had been sitting on the grass Sarah caught sight of a sign in front of the tree, and walked closer to read what it said. After scanning the words she called out to her sisters.

"Did you two read this sign? It says three sisters - triplets - lived here and their parents planted this tree for them. Look, I'll read it out to you: 'This Elm Tree was planted by William and Sarah Bowen to commemorate the birth of their triplet daughters, Sarah Faith, Louisa Hope and Grace Charity. Born 1905.' How funny, we have the same names as they do," Sarah said excitedly. "Maybe we've got some psychic connection to this place," she added.

"Oh, you and your stupid psychic mumbo jumbo. Just because that palm reader saw something in your hand, it doesn't mean anything. They just make all that stuff up you know," Hope scoffed.

"It seemed very real when she told me my life was about to change. I didn't tell her we were coming to Australia, or even that we were travelling," Sarah replied quickly.

"I'm more interested in how triplets born here in 1905 managed to survive. There can't have been that many triplets around Launceston nearly 100 years ago. That poor mother!" Grace interjected. "Come on, let's have a look around before Aunt Mary starts sending out a search party."

Sarah could not stop thinking about the peacock she knew

she had seen and the three girls from the gorge who shared the McKinnon sisters' names. Surely that couldn't just be a coincidence. The palm reader had said her life would change during this trip. Maybe what she had seen that afternoon was all part of what was going to happen.

Early the following morning Sarah woke with an indescribable sense that she needed to visit the elm tree. As the first rays of golden light pierced the pale pink sky Sarah dressed quietly and snuck out the back door, checking quickly that she wasn't being followed. A brisk walk down the hill saw her back at the tree within minutes. She sat, eyes closed, against its cool and solid trunk and meditated for an hour before duty called her back to her aunt's home. Since the other three women had only just started to stir, Sarah's secret was safe. Every time she thought about the tree and the gorge triplets Sarah felt her stomach flutter. She knew everything was about to change.

The sun hung low behind the Cataract Gorge late that afternoon and the three sisters were buzzing in anticipation of what might happen that night. The twins hoped they would meet two handsome men who would take their mind off the fact that their little sister would be with them. Sarah hoped she could find another magical piece to her psychic puzzle.

Despite their eagerness to get to The Basin, the grassy area the McKinnon sisters had explored the day before was already crowded when they arrived for the festival. None of them knew the bands on the bill, but they didn't care because it was a night to play away from their matronly aunt. Hope and Grace were walking a step ahead of Sarah. She quickened her pace to catch up, but tripped on her shoelace and stopped to do it up.

Feeling rushed now, Sarah straightened up hurriedly and promptly walked straight into someone. Embarrassed and flustered, Sarah looked up to apologise, but was rendered speechless by the striking blue of the eyes staring into hers. The man in front of Sarah grabbed her arm and helped her stand upright, moving her out of the path of the crowd at the same time. She tried to thank him, but was still mute, unable to stop staring into his deep blue eyes.

"Are you ok?" the man's words jolted Sarah from the spell she had fallen under.

"Um, yes. I think so. I didn't hurt myself, I was just retying my lace," Sarah stuttered.

"Oh good. Well I'm Nick. Are you here with anyone?"

"I'm Sarah, and I'm here with my sisters, but they've left me."

"That's OK, you can sit with me and my mates until you find them."

"No, no I should find them. They might be worried about me and we promised our aunt we'd stay together," Sarah smiled apologetically.

"Well, it's my loss. I was hoping I'd meet a pretty girl tonight and one just happens to bowl me over. If you change your mind we're sitting over by the rocks," Nick said, pointing to a rocky outcrop to the left of the path.

"Thanks, I'll think about it," Sarah said, and then suddenly felt an incredible urge to say yes. "Actually, I can find my sisters later. I'd love to sit with you."

Stunned at herself for being so forward, Sarah allowed Nick to take her hand and guide her through the excited throng. He motioned for her to sit on the tartan rug that covered one of the larger rocks and sat down beside her.

"Everyone, this is Sarah. Sarah, this is everyone," Nick laughed, and his friends jeered and poked him in the ribs. "Hey, stop it. Sarah and I had a collision and, being the gentleman I am, I thought I should make sure she's OK while she waits for her sisters," he smirked.

"Yeah right," one of the friends said, and winked at Sarah as he offered her a beer.

"No thanks, I don't really like beer," she said.

"That's OK, we've got wine and water too," Nick said, squeezing her hand.

Sarah felt a bolt of electricity shoot up her arm at his touch. Suddenly her skin felt charged and she wondered if this was what the palm reader had seen. Always the shy girl at school, Sarah had felt more at home in the library than joining her friends who, as their school years dwindled, had started talking to boys one by one. The only boys she spoke to were those in her book group, and they were just as awkward around the opposite sex as she was. This was definitely uncharted territory, Sarah thought as the first band started playing a song. Nick reached out to Sarah and grabbed her hand, pulling her close to him. Sarah laid her head on his shoulder and drank in his scent: a heady mixture of aftershave, musky sweat and beer. There was nowhere else Sarah wanted to be. Nick's embrace felt like home.

The rest of the night sped past in a blur of hand holding, sipping wine and laughter. Sarah knew she wouldn't be able to answer any questions about the bands or the music they played, but she could tell anyone who asked the exact shade of Nick's eyes, that he had a wry sense of humour and was a gentleman.

When Sarah had started to fade, Nick walked her back to her aunt's, sheepishly asking her if they could meet at the Gorge the following day. Not caring what her sisters' or aunt's plans were, Sarah responded immediately with: "Definitely! Meet me under the elm at 10," pecked Nick on the cheek, hurriedly opened the door and ran inside.

Exhausted from her early morning and very eventful night, Sarah collapsed, fully clothed, on her bed and fell into a deep sleep. Refreshed, she woke early the next morning and saw her sisters were still sleeping. Sarah heard her aunt in the kitchen and went to join her, suddenly feeling ravenous. As she put some bread in the toaster, her aunt boiled the kettle and asked how her night was.

"Magical," Sarah answered, gazing up at the ceiling.

Her aunt laughed and said: "I know that look. You've met a young man, haven't you? I don't think your mother will approve of that, but I suppose nothing will come of it since you're going home in a few months."

"We'll see," Sarah smiled. "I'm meeting him at the Gorge this morning."

"You be careful Sarah. Make sure you don't do anything stupid," her Aunt Mary said, concern spreading across her face.

"I won't Aunt Mary, don't worry," she said, and buttered her toast distractedly.

By a few minutes to 10 Sarah was waiting eagerly under the elm tree, anxious to see Nick wasn't a figment of her imagination. The couple met at the same time, same place every morning Nick wasn't working at the Gorge Tea Rooms for the next two months.

They talked for hours as they walked along the well-trodden bush tracks that looped through the incredible rock formation. Each took turns bringing a picnic to share and, by the end of the first week, Nick was making plans to visit Sarah in Scotland in three months.

"I'm taking a year off before I go to university and I've saved up enough money from my casual job to come to Scotland. I've already told my parents I'm going to do it," he said, his blue eyes flashing with excitement.

Sarah didn't want the two months to end, but before she knew it she and her sisters were packing their suitcases for the long trip home.

"What are you going to do without lover boy?" Hope teased.

"He's taking us to the airport in his dad's car, so you'd better be nice or I'll tell him to leave you behind!" Sarah said proudly.

"I hope you don't think we're going to hang around and watch you two get all soppy while you say goodbye," Grace quipped.

"I don't care what you do, but I'll be making the most of every second I have with Nick. I love him," Sarah said, and left the room with her suitcase.

Nick parked his father's car outside the blue cottage. The McKinnon sisters said their final goodbyes to their aunt and soon they were on the way to the airport. Sarah put her hand on Nick's left thigh and squeezed his leg as he drove along the Midlands Highway towards Evandale. They discussed plans for his upcoming trip and Hope and Grace chatted together about the homecoming party they expected to be guests of honour at when they returned to Skye.

"I'll write to you every week and I'll be there to kiss you before you know it," Nick said as he hugged Sarah one last time, only letting her go when the final boarding call for their flight to Sydney sounded.

"I love you," she mouthed and waved, putting her hands in her pocket to touch the handkerchief containing three elm seeds.

~~~

Two weeks after her return to Skye, Sarah hadn't heard from Nick. She was certain there was a reason. After all, she knew their romance had been destined by a higher being and he had told her he loved her many times. As she had done every day since being home, Sarah opened the handkerchief and looked at the three seeds she had collected from the Cataract Gorge elm she and Nick had used as their meeting spot. She gently touched their papery thin wings and heard the phone ring.

Her mother's voice answered the call and she quickly called to her youngest daughter: "Sarah, there's an Australian lady on the phone for you. Hurry up, it's an international call." Puzzled, Sarah took the phone receiver and tentatively spoke: "Hello?"

"Sarah? Is this Sarah McKinnon? It's Mrs Murphie, Eileen Murphie. I'm Nick's mum."

"Oh, hello Mrs Murphie. How are you? How is Nick?"

"I wish I was calling under better circumstances, honey. There's been an accident and…"

~~~

"Mum, mum! Where are you? I'm starving!" Her son's voice pierced her memories and Sarah was pulled away from her thoughts and back to the present. She hurriedly got to her feet and put her hand to her face, feeling the hot tears rolling down her cheeks.

"Mum, when are you cooking our dinner? I'm dying of

starvation," the boy asked emphatically.

"Now. I'm coming now Nicky," Sarah stammered, wiping her tears with the back of her hand and turning to smile at her son.

EVOLUTION

Wishing:

Bound and alone, I wait and watch as the years come and go.

How I wish I could soar like the colourful two-winged creature
who escapes her own prison and graciously flutters away.

How I wish I could run like those magnificent beasts, snorting
and foaming as they pass me by without a glance.

How I wish I did not feel the pain of being stripped of my coat,
leaving me bare and vulnerable for the cold months of winter.

Being:

With thanks, I sit amazed as the morning light awakens the sky.

How lucky I am to plant my roots, weaving and turning, pushing
deeper and deeper into the damp, dark soil.

How lucky I am to enjoy the laughter and calling of my feathered
friends as they wake with the sunrise and start to play.

How lucky I am to feel the warmth of the setting sun and the
cool light of the moon, as I grow taller and stronger with each
passing day.

Giving:

In silence, I sit and wonder at the essence of being still.

How I love to feel the biting, scratching and playing of the tiny
crawling creatures who like to call me home.

How I love to feel my breath reach out to the sky and know that I
am giving all that I am to nourish the earth.

How I love those squawking, nesting angels who feed and strip
me of my coat, leaving me bare and vulnerable for the cold
months of winter.

by Tracey Regan

A chapter from the upcoming novel
The Final Solution
- Tracey Regan

Kelly - 1993

As the plane hit turbulence, Kelly opened her eyes wide, and remembered where she was and the daunting task ahead of her. She looked down at the tiny rows of boxes. Street after street of houses joined together, never knowing where one house stopped and another began, snaking around in swirling patterns of grey. She had travelled to London once before as a teenager, when her parents had brought her to see her aging uncle before he died, and she was struck by the same feeling of greyness as she had felt then.

The plane touched the tarmac at Heathrow and a wave of loneliness swept over her. She was already missing her daughter, but her loneliness was much deeper than that. She was worried about Daisy, but that's what Mum's do when they only have one child, and at fifteen they think they know it all. She had left Daisy in New York with her grandmother, much to her disgust, "but Mom, I really don't need a babysitter, you can trust me. You're only going up the coast for a couple of days. I can call you if there's a problem." They ended up having a huge fight about it, but in the end, she'd told her she was going away with a boyfriend for the weekend, and didn't want to have to worry that she would be ok.

Both her mother and Daisy had been so excited. They so wanted her to find someone special and stop obsessing over ghosts of the past. But they should have guessed there was no boyfriend and instead she'd jumped on a plane and headed to London because of some tiny article she'd seen in the paper. Every day for years, she'd bought a copy of the Wall Street Journal and scanned the pages for any story that might relate to Daisy's father. Kelly was the first to admit her obsession was out of control.

The first few years of Daisy's life she had tried to forget Paul Connors and ignore any feelings she had. It had been fairly easy at first, but as Daisy got older, and it was obvious that she wasn't physically developing at a 'normal' rate, she'd tried everything to find Paul. She needed to find a reason for Daisy's slower growth rate. None of the many doctors she had seen could explain it, and after a while no-one cared. She was developing a little slowly physically, sure, but she was healthy and happy and her mental capacity didn't seem affected. In fact, she was highly intelligent. Kelly had become obsessive despite doctors, family and friends telling her there was nothing to worry about. Kelly couldn't give it up! She had paid crazy amounts of money for private detectives and spent hours pouring through financial papers from around the world. Paul had been a regular contributor to the Wall Street Journal while he had lived in New York and Kelly was convinced that was her only connection to him. She had employed private detectives around the world with just an old photo, hoping he might be working in a top corporate job of a major bank, somewhere, but it seemed that once he left New York he had literally disappeared.

But last Monday when she briefly skimmed through the paper, a short article caught her eye; a new appointment and a picture of Tom Peterson. It looked so much like him, she had gasped when she'd seen it. She called Sid, her detective contact in London, to go track him down and get a photo to her as soon as possible. The photo she received via fax just one day later really did take her breath away. It was without doubt Daisy's father, but not only that, fifteen years on and he looked almost exactly the same, but he had always looked after himself and seemed younger than his years .

She had booked her flight right then and arranged for Sid to meet her at the airport. As she collected her luggage, she felt completely overwhelmed and even light-headed. Despite all the years of looking for Paul, or Tom, or whatever his damn name was, she had never really thought about what she would say when she came face to face with him. She had been so obsessed with the idea of finding him, but for some reason she'd blocked out the thought of the conversation she would have to tell him about his daughter, when she saw him for the first time in fifteen years.

Her bag felt full of lead, despite her only bringing a few essentials and she stumbled a little as she made her way to customs and the 'nothing to declare' channel. She told herself it was her flustered and dishevelled appearance that caught the eye of the customs officer, but it was typical that they would pick her out to go through her luggage. She'd never met Sid before, but she could imagine him waiting for her, her name written on a flimsy piece of paper, waiting while passenger after passenger walked straight passed him.

She'd used him many times over the last few years and he always seemed just a little gruff and rather impatient at the other end of the phone, so she was really going to get on his good side now, keeping him waiting while the customs officer slowly went through every single piece of her luggage. He patted down the pockets of her jeans, pulled out everything from her toiletries bag, and insisted on making idle chit chat. She just wanted to get out of there and get Sid to take her to Paul's workplace so she could find out what the hell was going on with their daughter. "How long are you 'ere for luv?" asked the customs officer as he grabbed her passport.

"What? Sorry, what did you say?" Kelly was in a daze.

"How long? What are you here for? When do you leave?" Her mind was so distant, she could barely hear him. "Miss? Do you speak English?"

"Yes, sorry. I'm just here for the weekend. Catching up with an old friend I haven't seen in years," Kelly's eyes filled with tears and just for a moment he smiled softly at her.

"It's been a long flight hasn't it? Too long for just the weekend I reckon." He handed back her passport, "well it can only get better from here right? Sorry to have delayed you, Ms Foster. Have a fantastic weekend in London and I hope your old friend really appreciates the journey you've made."

She smiled but his words were swirling around her head. "It can only get better from here." She passed through the arrivals gate into a swarm of happiness; families hugging, long lost lovers holding each other and tiny children running into the arms of their grandparents. She saw a line of chauffeurs and drivers all holding their signs high, shifting from one foot to the next, laughing or complaining about how their customer was sure to be a 'pain in the arse,' but none of those signs had her name on it.

Sid had promised he would be there, she was paying him a fortune after all, but maybe he'd got tired of waiting. Maybe he was outside smoking, or just decided she wasn't worth it. She didn't want to be alone in this crowd, trying to work out where to go and what to do next. Sid had told her he'd already booked her hotel, but she had no idea where. She pushed through the crowd, pacing through the terminal, checking those signs again and again, but after half an hour, she decided it was time to give Sid's office a call. She had to buy a disgusting cup of coffee just to get change for the phone. She turned her bag inside out searching for the piece of paper she'd written Sid's details on, but it took the hot, sweet bitterness of the coffee burning her tongue to calm her enough to find it. "It can only get better from here," she repeated over and over but for some reason her hands were shaking as she dialled the number to Sid's office. She just had a feeling in the pit of her stomach that something wasn't right. She felt like the whole world was watching her, judging her but she knew she was just worried about her meeting with Paul.

The first time she called Sid's office, the phone just rang and rang until she decided to hang up. She tried again but the people in the queue behind her were tutting and complaining so she just walked away sipping slowly at her coffee, before going back to the end of the queue. Kelly queued four times before someone finally picked up. She could hear the sound of muffled sobs as Catherine, Sid's assistant who she knew fairly well from previous conversations, answered the phone.

"Oh my God," said Kelly, "What's the matter? Are you OK?"

"We just had some bad news this morning, can I help you?" sobbed the poor girl on the other end of the phone.

"Catherine, it's Kelly, from New York. I'm just at Heathrow waiting for Sid but he's not here. Has something happened?"

There was silence, and then a sigh, before Catherine choked out the words, "Sid was in a car accident this morning Kelly. I'm so sorry. With all the drama I forgot you were arriving today..."

"Is he alright? What happened?" Kelly felt a tightness in her chest.

"Well, the police haven't said much, but he, um, he didn't make it through surgery. We still don't really know what happened." Catherine sobbed for a moment, then remembered she was on the phone. "Hey have you got all the details of your hotel and stuff, you'll probably want to go get some sleep or something."

"I'm so sorry about Sid, that must be devastating for you. Thanks though, if you can give me the hotel details that would great. And I'll give you a call tomorrow for all the other information."

"Ok." Kelly could hear the shuffling of papers and the sound of Catherine's gentle sobs as she waited patiently, knowing that Catherine wouldn't be there tomorrow, so she had to get as much information out of her as possible, despite the terrible circumstances.

"The hotel is called The Moorgate Hotel. It's near Moorgate underground station. It's just up the road from where your Mr. Peterson works."

"Where does he work, Catherine? What's his company?" Kelly interjected quickly. She could hear the shuffling of papers again as Catherine muttered, "It's called Schroders I think, look I gotta go Kelly. Good Luck."

Catherine had hung up before Kelly could say anymore. She felt her legs shake a little, as she leaned into the perspex shield separating the phones and held the handset into her chest, grabbing with both hands, as if it were keeping her upright. There was a bit of tutting and back chat from the queue as she placed the handset back in it's place, grabbed her bags and tried to find someplace she could sit down and collect her thoughts. Sid was dead! She knew it was wrong but she just kept thinking how difficult her task was going to be without him.

She decided she would make her way to the hotel, but she didn't have the strength to take the 'underground'. And besides she didn't have to pay Sid now. The thought made her feel guilty on top of all the other overwhelming feelings she was experiencing. As she went to stand, her legs buckled under her, and a wall of blackness hit her as she fell to the floor. When she opened her eyes she was surrounded by a sea of faces. Some were obviously concerned, others just gawking, so many voices asking the same question, "Is she alright? What's happened? Someone get a doctor." Hearing the babble of the voices was like she was underwater and couldn't reach the surface.

The airport police were quickly clearing the crowd and Kelly sat up, rubbing a small bump that she could feel forming on the back of her head. "I'm alright, really I am," she said to the policeman who was helping her to her feet. "You need to see a doctor, Miss. A bump on the head and loss of consciousness means you might have concussion, you gotta get it checked out."

"I just need a taxi to get to my hotel. Please. I'll be fine honestly. I'll go to a doctor if I need to later."

He tutted and shook his head a lot as he escorted her to the taxi rank and helped her into a taxi ahead of the queue that snaked back through to the doors indicating what would have been a very long wait.

The trip to her hotel in the taxi took just over an hour, in stop-start traffic. She stared out of the window at the grey, dirty streets as they drove away from the airport and that feeling of greyness was like a huge cloak enveloping her. But as they got closer to the City that feeling gave way to excitement and hopefulness, as the elegant, grand and historical buildings lifted her mood, and she even saw a little sunshine break through the clouds.

By the time she reached her hotel she was feeling a lot better. She went straight for the telephone directory to find out where she could find 'Schroders'. She was surprised to find there were three different offices in central London. She didn't have time to waste. She quickly showered, changed and ordered some room service. She hadn't realised how hungry she was and that had probably contributed to her feinting earlier.

She stared at herself in the mirror and smiled. "Not quite the Kelly from 1978, but beautiful just the same." She was a beautiful woman, and although the years of worry had taken their toll, she still stood out in a crowd. She was going to wear her bright red jacket, but thought better of it. Her jacket made her look amazing, but maybe she needed to be a little inconspicuous, after all, she still had no idea how she would deal with seeing Paul, or even if she could find him.

The receptionist gave her directions to the Schroders' offices and she discovered there was an office closeby. Catherine had said she was staying 'just up the road', so with naive anticipation she headed off, thinking she would just wait outside or in the foyer, or even go in to the office reception and ask to see him. When she arrived there a little over five minutes later, her courage had disappeared and she stood on the opposite side of the road, just staring at the entrance to the building. She stood there on the crowded street, people rushing past, even bumping into her it was that busy, as she shrank back against the building.

By the time she looked at her watch, she realised she'd been there for over an hour, just staring at the entrance. She had decided she should just leave, but suddenly the street became even busier if that was even possible. It was 5pm and all around her, and including the Schroders building opposite, hundreds of people were pouring out into the street, like a flood, flowing in the direction of the underground. She thought she might get swept up in the tide, but she pushed herself hard into the wall and just watched as people swarmed past her without a glance, their grey faces, looking down at the grey pavement, moving as one.

She continued to watch the entrance of the Schroders building, but her view was so obscured she was sure he could easily have left without her noticing. That's if he even worked at this building. She looked down at her watch again. 5.35. More office workers surged from the buildings onto the already crushing street.

As she lifted her gaze, it was like a lightning strike as she saw him walk out from the building. The only man she had ever loved, her obsession for the last ten years. She started to run, against the tide, even pushing people aside. She could barely breathe as she saw him on the opposite side of the road. It was like she could feel him. She could feel her energy so connected to his, and in that moment she saw him stop and turn in her direction. Did he see her? She felt like their eyes had met, but she couldn't be sure. She called his name, but the traffic noise was just too loud. He began walking again, but she could see him looking around.

She was pushing through the crowd, but it seemed hopeless, there were just so many people and she was desperate to cross the road. As she got close to the curb, it was the traffic that was stopping her. With the crowd all around her, it took a moment for Kelly to realise that someone was holding her. She felt a vice-like grip around her arm, a sharp sting to the back of her neck, and a push on her already limp body. The blackness was not quite instant. She saw the fear and instant panic in the driver's eyes and heard the hysterical screams of the people who watched her fall under the wheels of the bus.

<center>~~~</center>

Daisy stared down at the letter in her hand. She had not spoken for two months. She couldn't find her voice. Her mother was dead. Knocked down on a London street. What was she even doing there? And why? Why had she kept it a secret? She would never forget how she felt on the day of the funeral. She had never felt so alone. The police had said it was just a terrible traffic accident, but Daisy knew deep down there was something more. Especially now she had the letter. She would find the answers. Her life's purpose would be to make sure her mother didn't die without justice. And she would have her revenge.

The Sweetest Gift
- Tracey Regan

Phyllis Daley liked to chat. Unfortunately not everyone liked to chat with Phyllis. It was nothing new for her. She knew a lot of people judged her on her appearance and what she liked to call her 'old people' smell. She tried to mask it with lavender water and expensive perfume, but sometimes she wondered if that just added to the problem.

She was very particular about her appearance. Over the years she had collected a fantastic wardrobe and she had items dating back to the 1940's. Amazingly her 'size' hadn't changed over all that time, and in the last five years she had made it a priority to wear those clothes, though she did stop short of wearing her sixties mini dresses with the thigh high boots. She knew she had looked fabulous in them years ago but didn't think it would be quite appropriate these days.

Certainly not appropriate for her train trips into Perth every Monday, Wednesday and Friday from her home in Mandurah. She liked to get the first early morning train so she could move around and find people to chat to. The hour long trip was a perfect time to chat. She would chat whether people liked it or not. Today she was wearing a 1950's rocker dress. Of course, she had all the accessories and her make-up was done perfectly. She had struggled with the choice of shoes, but opted to wear the pair she had bought especially for this dress, even though they were a little high.

She smiled with the memory of herself in her mid-20's. What a time that had been. Thank goodness she still had her memories. The few friends she had left did not always have that luxury.

As she got on to the train and parked herself in her usual corner seat, she hugged her big heavy bag to her chest. It was particularly heavy today. It contained everything that meant anything to her.

As people began getting on to the train she realised she didn't look like a lady in the later stages of life is supposed to look. She knew she must have looked quite a sight! Nobody wanted to sit near her and there was certainly no eye contact despite the fact that she made a point of smiling at everyone who got on. Sadly, this morning it was not reciprocated. Although she caught the train at the same time three days a week, there was no-one she recognised yet this morning.

With only one seat left in the carriage, the one next to her, she smiled as a young teenage boy hesitated before finally deciding to take the seat. He had his underpants showing with his jeans pulled down as low as they could go and Phyllis tutted and shook her head. "Why do you wear your jeans like that? You're showing everyone your underpants you know."

"What's it to you?" he mumbled under his breath.

"Well I'm interested in fashion. Just wondering what makes you want to look like that."

"I could ask you the same question." He thought about getting up and moving away. Phyllis flinched a little at his remark but knew she was the last person who should judge people on appearance.

"Do you like cats?" Phyllis asked with a smile. "I have five of them, you know."

"Look crazy cat lady, I don't want to talk to you about your cats. OK. I don't want to talk to you at all. I just want to sit quietly and get to Perth without any distraction. Is that alright with you?"

"OK OK. I get the message. Your parents obviously never

taught you any manners. You're supposed to respect your elders you know." Phyllis carried on but she was now addressing the whole carriage, "Young people today just don't know how to be polite. When I was a teenager my parents would belt me if I spoke to my elders in the way young people do today. Not that I'm saying the modern world is a bad place. There's just no respect like there was in the old days. No respect at all."

Phyllis noticed the entire carriage was avoiding looking at her. Was she causing a disturbance? Not at all. She was just making conversation, but she could see she was making people uncomfortable, and not one person in that part of the carriage was interested in her opinion. They were all worried the crazy lady was going to start trying to talk to them. The young man next to her had put in his earphones and was playing his music so everyone could hear. Surely that was more of a disturbance than her wanting to chat, she thought.

Phyllis wanted to find one of her regular chatters. There were several people on the train who did have time for her and she needed to find them. She stood up in her high shoes and overbalanced with her huge bag. She was pretty sure she stood on a few toes but no-one acknowledged her as she pushed past. "Excuse me. Excuse me please."

She pushed through to the next part of the carriage and was happy to see a familiar face. She was glad Sarah was on the train this morning.

"Good morning, Phyllis. Here, have my seat. You're looking fabulous this morning. Where did you get that amazing outfit, may I ask?

"Hi, Sarah. It's lovely to see you. Well this little number I bought in Carnaby Street in 1954, the same year I met Elvis. In fact, I wore this outfit when I met him."

Sarah raised her eyebrows. "You've never told me about that before Phyllis, have you been holding out on me? What was he like?"

"Oh you know, pretty quiet actually. I had drinks with him in his hotel room, but the room was so packed with his entourage, it was hard to talk much. I really liked him though." Phyllis could see that Sarah was just humouring her. She never really believed anything Phyllis told her, but it was fun running over old memories.

"So Sarah tell me, what's happening with you and the kids. How did Johnny go in his footy game this weekend?"

They talked for a while, but Phyllis had an agenda. She needed to find at least two more people on the train and she was worried she would run out of time. She interrupted Sarah while she was telling Phyllis about her daughter's gymnastic competition.

"Sorry Sarah, it's been lovely to see you this morning but I have to find another friend on the train. Before I go I want to give you something, but only if you promise not to open it until you get home, ok?" Phyllis pulled a small jar from her big bag. It was beautifully hand-painted, with a big "Thank You" on the glass, and was filled with gummy bears.

"Promise me? Promise you won't open it 'til later."

"Sure luv. I promise. How did you know gummy bears are my favourite? This is so cool. Thanks Phyllis."

"No thank you. It's been lovely chatting to you about your family. I still don't understand why you work in Perth every day, polishing brass at that silly gentlemen's club. I'm sure as soon as you polish the banisters those executive lawyers and doctors smear their fingerprints all over it. Seems like such a thankless task.

"Well I've done it for years Phyllis and it's convenient you know. Rod looks after the kids in the morning and takes them to school and goes to work afternoon shift, and I get home to pick up the kids. It just works.

I wish you could give up your job and spend a bit more time with your family. You probably hardly ever see your husband."

"Yeah that would be lovely, but I'd have to win lotto first hey," she smiled.

"What about that idea you have for starting your own business? You've shown me your designs, they're really good you know."

"Blimey that's me just dreaming. What's the gift for anyway?"

"Well I'm going into a home today so I won't be travelling into town anymore."

Sarah realised she didn't even know why Phyllis travelled into town three days a week and felt a pang of guilt. In two years of chatting to her, she knew nothing about her except her made up stories of travel to exotic places and famous celebrities. As Phyllis stood up Sarah gave her a big hug. "Good luck Phyllis. It's been lovely talking with you. Thanks for listening to me carry on about my kids. I've really enjoyed listening to your stories."

"Bye Sarah. Thanks for being polite and letting me chat with you." Phyllis handed her the jar. "Now remember, don't open it until you get home."

Phyllis stood up in her silly shoes and stumbled her way slowly through the carriage. She was looking for Ernie. Ernie always had time for her. He made her feel special. She wished she was twenty years younger as she was pretty sure he would've been interested in her then. Her heart skipped a little beat when she saw him.

"Mrs. D. Wow you look amazing today." Ernie stood up and helped her into his seat. "Your make-up's fabulous, you don't look a day over 70! What's the special occasion?"

"Well, Ernie, it's my last day on the train today. They're making me go into a 'special facility'. They say I can't look after myself. What rubbish. And they won't let me take my cats. I don't know what I'm going to do without them." A little tear appeared in the corner of her eyes and she was cross with herself for letting her emotion show.

"Damn it Phyllis, that's bloody outrageous." His strong cockney accent was accentuated when he was angry. "Who have I gotta to speak to? I'm gonna sort this out for you. It's not like you've lost your marbles or anything. You get yourself into town three days a week, and you take your pills every day. How can they do this to you?"

"It's alright Ernie. I guess it's the right time. They're worried I might hurt myself. It's just my cats I'm worried about."

"Well, you've got my number if there's anything I can do to 'elp ya luv. Do you want me to try and find homes for them."

"Well if you can, but you've got enough to worry about Ernie. How's everything going?"

"Oh we've still got little Danny living with us. Margaret loves taking care of him, but he is exhausting her. You know little kids, always on the go and talking ALL DAY. He doesn't stop. Ha. I don't know where he gets the gift of the gab from," he laughed out loud. "He turned three last month, he's just the cutest little button," he leant down and whispered in her ear. "Kelly's still in rehab but she seems to be getting better, it just means I'm going to have to work well into my retirement to pay for it all. I thought I'd be done by now and travelling 'round Aus in a campervan."

"Well when you get to my age and Kelly is well and happy, you'll appreciate it."

"Don't you have any family Phyllis?"

"No. I was married a couple of times but just not able to have kids. Don't feel sorry for me though, I've had an amazing life."

"How could I feel sorry for you? From what you've told me you've been to more countries than I can count and hey, you've met Nelson Mandela and JFK."

"Yep, it's been awesome." Phyllis gave him a wink. "Hey, I've got to get moving. There's someone else I want to catch up with before we get to Perth and I'm running out of time. I have something for you though Ernie." Phyllis pulled another beautifully painted jar from her bag.

"Lemon bon-bons. My favourite. How did you know that?"

"I'm not just snoozing when you talk you know. I do listen. You told me they were your favourite a long time ago.

He bent down and kissed her cheek. "Well Thank You. You have my number, so don't be a stranger. Give me a call if you want to chat. You can come over to our place for lunch or dinner one weekend."

"I'd like that Ernie. Thank you," said Phyllis as she struggled to get to her feet. "Take care of your family now, won't you?"

Ernie lifted her up in his strong arms and gave her a hug. "I'll treasure my bon-bons Mrs. D."

"I know you will Ernie." Phyllis had a smile on her face and a tear in her eye as she continued down the carriage, but didn't look back.

Through the doors into the next carriage she could see another familiar face. She had to move fast because she knew Sam would be getting off at the next stop. Her heavy bag was bumping into people as she passed. There were plenty of grumbled remarks as she apologized but pushed her way through the crowd, stumbling and stepping on toes.

She must have looked quite stressed by the time she got to him, as his eyes were full of concern.

"Phyllis? What's going on? Are you OK? Are you sure you should be wearing those shoes? Haven't you got a spare pair of thongs in that Mary Poppins bag of yours?" He held her strongly under her free arm, as she steadied herself.

"Thank you Sam, I'm fine. Really. I just needed to catch up with you before you get off. It's my last day on the train today and I want to give you something." She pulled the painted jar from her bag.

Sam laughed loudly, "Black Jacks! I haven't seen them in years. Well thank you so much Phyllis. What d'you mean, 'last day'?"

"I'm struggling by myself Sam. I'm going into a home today. I did put up a bit of a fight, but it's not like it's prison. I still get to come and go as I please. I just get some help with stuff that's all."

"So does this mean I won't see you again and hear all your wonderful stories? Let me give you my number and you can call me if you have some free time on the weekend. We can catch up for coffee." Sam handed her his business card and held her hand.

"I'd like that Sam. Please tell me your son is doing well."

"He is Phyllis. After three months in hospital we're taking him home at the end of this week. As you know, Tash has spent the whole time there with him. She's really looking forward to bringing him home. Are you going to the hospital today? Maybe you could pop in and see them. I know they'd love to chat with you."

"I will Sam. I will go and see them." The train pulled in to the station and Sam gave Phyllis a big hug. "Take care of the Black Jack's Sam. I painted that jar myself you know."

As he got off the train he smiled and waved, but both of them knew they would never see each other again.

She had only two more stops to go but she was struggling to stand. The journey had exhausted her and her shoes and bag didn't help matters. She wished she had thought more about her shoe choice or as Sam had suggested, put some thongs in her bag. Suddenly she remembered she had some slippers in her bag and decided it was the only option. They might not match her dress but that was a chance she would have to take.

She looked at the beautiful young lady dressed in an Alex Perry outfit sitting in the 'saved for the elderly' seat behind her, her long blonde hair draped over her book protecting her from the stares of the men in the carriage.

"Excuse me, Miss. Would you mind if I sat down. I really need to get out of these shoes."

Her face burned bright red as she got up without saying a word or even looking at her. "Thanks lovely, I was really struggling there." She began emptying her big bag onto her lap. She still had lots of glass jars on the top of the bag and was having a bit of trouble making sure they were safe. The elderly man sitting next to her looked up.

"Would you like some help? Just let me put this iPad away and I'll hold some of your jars for you."

"Thanks that would be great. Do you like cats?" she said as she began handing him the contents of her bag. "I have five of them you know."

"Well I prefer dogs to be honest. What are you doing with all these beautifully painted jars filled with sweets?"

"It's my last day on the train today and at the hospital, so I'm giving them as presents to the people who have been nice to me."

"Well that's a lovely idea. Though I'm sure many people would consider just knowing you to be a good enough gift. I'm sure you would have some amazing stories to tell. I'm David by the way."

"Phyllis. It's lovely to meet you David. Now I just need to find my slippers and I can put all of this away again."

"You look tired Phyllis. Do you need some help getting to the hospital this morning? Oh my God, what's this?" David held up a metal Cadillac car emblem.

"Well there is a good story that goes with that," laughed Phyllis, "if you've got the time I will share it with you."

" I'm sure it's a fantastic story," David laughed. "You can tell me on the way to the hospital. I'm really early for work so if it's ok with you, I'd like to help you there. I'll hold your very heavy bag for you."

"You are so kind, David and very polite. It's lovely to meet someone with such beautiful manners. I stole that Cadillac emblem you know. I'm so naughty aren't I?" Phyllis laughed at the memory.

"It was back in the 60's. I drove an open-top Cadillac all the way down Route 66, in America, you know. When I finished the trip I had to take something to remember it by. I thought the car emblem was pretty cool. I've got all my treasures with me today." David held up a necklace. "That was a gift from Nelson Mandela. It's a traditional South African necklace. My husband, rest his soul, was a foreign minister so I got to travel the world and meet some amazing people."

"That is so cool," said David as the train pulled into the station and he stood up helping Phyllis to her feet. She was much more comfortable in her slippers.

"I have to catch the bus David, but we have to catch the one with the right driver. I want to give my friend Chanelle one of my lolly jars."

Phyllis was so happy to find someone to listen to her stories, she chatted for ages. They sat at the bus stop for a while letting buses go past until the 'right' driver arrived. David helped Phyllis up on to the bus.

"David, I'll be alright from here. Chanelle drops me right at the door. But thanks for being so kind. I'd like to give you one of my hand-painted lolly jars if that's ok. Don't open it 'til you get home."

"Ok Phyllis, take care of yourself. And thanks for the lollies. I will keep the jar. It will remind me of our wonderful morning."

Phyllis got onto the bus and gave David a big smile. She turned to Chanelle, "I've been waiting for you for ages. Lucky I had a lovely man to talk to. I won't be coming into Perth again Chanelle, so I want to give you one of my hand-painted lolly jars," she handed over the jar. "Don't open it until you get home ok."

By the time Phyllis got to the Children's hospital, she was

exhausted, but she had a lot of lolly jars to drop off. For the last five years she had come to the hospital as a volunteer. She just sat and chatted to lots of people all day and then went home, but she knew she was just too old now and it was wearing her out. By mid-day she was ready for her appointment. She had handed out her jars to everyone on her list and her bag was so much lighter now, but she had one last jar to deliver. She had made an appointment with the Foundation director and was ushered into the board room by the secretary.

She was surprised to see that all the members of the board were there.

"I've come to let you know I won't be able to volunteer at the hospital anymore, but I have a special gift I'd like to give to the Foundation." She handed the jar to Elizabeth Keen, a committee member she'd come to know well over the years.

"Before we get to that Phyllis, we just want to say a huge Thank You for all that you've done for the hospital in recent years. Your donations have been invaluable and we are really going to miss your non-stop chattering around the place."

Everyone clapped and smiled and Phyllis felt a tear roll down her cheek. "Well, wait until you see what's in the lolly jar then! What am I going to do with my money now heh? I can't leave it to my cats can I?"

Elizabeth opened the jar and out fell a folded piece of paper. It was a bank cheque for two million dollars.

****

Sarah Stanton arrived home after picking up her children. They always drove her crazy after school, it was as if they hadn't eaten in days. She cut them up some fruit, but by the time she'd cut it they'd already raided the cupboard for lollies and chocolate biscuits. The little one had found the jar of gummy bears Phyllis had given her on the train.

She would miss Phyllis. Despite her being a little eccentric and wearing some pretty outrageous clothes for an eighty something year old, Sarah loved their chats and how knowledgeable she was about world events and places she'd been. As her daughter opened the jar a small folded piece of paper fell out. Sarah's eyes filled with tears as she opened the paper and found it was a bank cheque for the sum of one hundred thousand dollars.

Echoes of Ella
- Teena Raffa-Mulligan

My sister Ella's wedding day didn't turn out at all the way we'd planned. Right when she should have been walking down the aisle to promise to love Dean for ever, her wedding dress was still hanging in the wardrobe in its plastic cover. At my worst times I wanted to burn it. It wouldn't change what had happened, but at least it wouldn't be there to remind me I should have done my job better. What's the point of being someone's caretaker and guardian angel if you let them down at the time you're most needed?

I'd certainly had enough practice looking after Ella. After all, I'd been doing it almost my entire life and with my fourteenth birthday just weeks away I thought I had probably reached Olympic standard at big sister protection. Not that there was anything wrong with Ella. She was just a bit ditzy. A dreamer. Off in her own world most of the time and not really paying attention to what was going on in this one. So she needed someone to look after her. And that was me.

Then Dean turned up. Smart, funny, gorgeous and most important of all, rock-solid and sensible. Just the kind of guy my sister needed. It looked like my days of looking after Ella were almost over. I could get on with my own life.

But habits are hard to break. I hadn't done the official handover so I was still doing my job. I didn't slack off that sunny Saturday, even though I'd just had a text from my best friend Kate telling me the girls were all going to head down to Charlie's Beachside Cafe for a thick shake, mega muffins and a Help Lexie Lose Lover Boy planning session. It sounded fun and I knew my contribution to the campaign would be invaluable but I had a priority – house hunting with Ella and Dean. Let my off-with-the-fairies sister make an important decision like that? Not likely. Down to earth Dean might be, but all Ella had to do was smile and he wanted to give her the sun on a string to wear round her neck. My presence was vital to such an important undertaking, so I invited myself along.

"Haven't you got homework?" asked Ella. "Friends? A life?" I gave her my sweetest little sister smile.

"Yup times three. But I'm willing to put them all on hold. You need me. Who better to suss out all the shonky agents trying to sell you a lemon?"

Ella rolled her eyes at Dean and sighed dramatically. He patted me on the head.

"Just see you behave yourself, kiddo. If you're a really good girl and stay out of mischief we might buy you an ice cream on the way home."

It was my turn to roll my eyes – at him. He thinks I'm an ordinary kid sister. Hasn't got a clue how often I've rescued Ella from disaster. Guardian Angel, first class, that's me. Teenage nerd is just a disguise.

"So..."

Before they could have second thoughts about letting me join the home hunt, I bounced into the back of Dean's cute yellow jeep – Ella's choice of course, not his. He wanted the practical sedan that used gas rather than petrol and would have room in the back for bassinettes and car seats when the little ones started to arrive. See what I mean? He's hopeless when Ella sets her heart on something. But I'm getting sidetracked. Back to that Saturday…

"What's the plan?" I asked. "Do we have a list of possibilities?"

Ella got that weird look in her eyes, which gives me the shivers because I know from experience that no good can come of it.

"I'll know it when I see it," she said. "Here." And she patted her heart. "Who needs a list?"

"I do." And Dean patted his pocket. "Don't worry, kid," he told me.

"Everything's under control. I've got the homes open list from the local paper and I've worked out our route. But first I thought we'd swing by that new display village they've been advertising on telly and check out the house and land packages they're offering."

What's that saying? The best laid plans? We didn't make it to the display village or any of the homes that were open for inspection that afternoon. We were heading along a back road through the bush that separates the older part of town from the new estate when Ella sat bolt upright and clutched Dean's arm.

"Stop!" He jammed on the brakes. "What?"

"There!" she said. "That's it!"

Dean had barely turned off the ignition before she was out of the car and dashing towards the house that had caught her attention.

"She can't be serious." Dean turned in the driver's seat and raised an eyebrow in my direction.   I shrugged. This was Ella. Who could say? But I was as stunned as he was.

The house was ancient and had clearly been empty for years. Neglected would be an understatement. It looked like it was waiting for the bulldozer, not new owners. No wonder the For Sale sign hanging off the front gate was faded and rusty. Who would want to buy such a monstrosity?

And yet we could feel Ella's excitement as she flung open the gate and rushed up the overgrown path to the rickety front steps. Shaking his head, Dean got out of the car and hurried after her.

I got out too. This was definitely a priority one, guardian angel assignment. What was Ella thinking?

"What do you think?" she asked Dean when he reached the front door.

I answered for him. "You're nuts. Absolutely."

At least she couldn't get in so her enthusiasm was bound to fizzle out once she'd looked in the windows and wandered round the yard. I sat down on the porch to wait. But I didn't even get the chance to take my iPod out of my pocket. She was trying the front door knob. And it opened. Would you believe it? Not even locked. And in she went, with Dean at her heels and me scurrying after them.

"You can't just walk in uninvited." Dean looked like he thought the trespass police were going to leap out from their hiding place at any moment and arrest him. I didn't feel all that comfortable either. But that was because of Ella. She was in raptures.

Anyone would have thought she'd just been given the pot of

gold at the end of the rainbow. She actually danced from room to room, pausing only long enough to lovingly stroke a wall or window sill, open and close a drawer or cupboard. And she positively glowed. Like someone had switched on a light. There was the tune, too. From the minute she walked into that house she was humming it, a melody that sounded like it should be familiar but wasn't. It spooked me. The whole thing did. And I know Dean felt the same.

We just wanted to get out of there, get out of this horrible house with its flaking paint, peeling wallpaper and torn curtains clinging to dirty windows. It was old and falling apart and we couldn't understand why Ella was so excited.

"It's everything I've ever dreamed of," she said. "Can't you see it? Red gingham at the kitchen windows, a tablecloth and cushions to match… A spice rack near the stove and a row of herbs in pots on the sill and more growing just outside the door… A veggie garden, of course, and a tyre swing on a rope hanging from a huge spreading fig tree in the yard. I'll make jam, lots of it. And the children will help. I can already hear them laughing. Listen…"

Her hands were clasped as if she was praying and she tilted her head to hear what we couldn't. We stared at each other and then at her.

She laughed. "You're kidding me. You must be able to hear them. They're outside playing."

I suddenly wished I'd worn my jacket. It was cold in here. I grabbed her arm.

"Come on, Ella, let's go."

"Yeah," said Dean. "This place gives me the creeps. Let's go and look at some normal houses."

He took her other arm. She shook us off and began to cry.

"No! I don't want another house. I want this one. I know it needs work but I can make it something beautiful. Please, Dean. I've never wanted anything so much in my life."

"Honey, be sensible. Just making it liveable would cost a small fortune. Besides, it probably isn't even worth fixing. Anyone with half a brain would flatten it and build a new house on the block."

But as I said, where Ella's concerned Dean loses his senses and within minutes he was promising to phone the agent, talk to the bank and get a quote for repairs.

I tried to get them to see reason but I might as well have saved my breath. When we finally shut the door on the place all I could hope was that Dean at least would return to sanity before they got themselves into a situation even a guardian angel couldn't put right.

As we got back in the car I felt such a sense of relief we'd got Ella out of there, as if she'd been at some terrible risk. I was mentally laughing the thought away when she suddenly pushed open the car door and began running back towards the house.

"I've left my bag inside," she yelled over her shoulder. I was after her in a flash. I knew I couldn't let her go back into that house.

But I didn't reach her in time. And much as I tried the knob the door wouldn't open for me. And as the tears ran down my cheeks and I called her name, I heard what she'd heard - the laughter of children. And her laughter joined theirs.

By the time Dean had used all of his strength to bash down the door the house was empty and still. No Ella. No children.

People don't just walk through a door and disappear into thin air. Well that's what I thought. Until Ella did. And one day I know another door will open and she'll walk through it and back into our lives. I just have to find the right door. So I wait...and watch...and listen for echoes of Ella.

The Final Hour   (A Screenplay)
- Ross Cameron

---

1. EXT. DUSK   1.

Open on an isolated cottage on a hill, overlooking town. It is just before dusk on a winter evening and the lights of the town twinkle in the gloom of the valley. A mid twenties man, **CONNER**, creeps up to a window and peers inside. He is wearing jeans and a tee shirt. The tee shirt is torn and covered in grime.

2. POV INTO COTTAGE   2.

A man in his seventies leaves his armchair and moves into the kitchen, a small dog follows on his heels.

3. EXT. DUSK. MID SHOT   3.

CONNER is about to tap on the window when there is the sound of an approaching car. Conner hesitates and turns.

4. EXT. DUSK. WIDE SHOT OF ROAD   4.

The headlights of the approaching car appear over the hill. The car is driving fast towards camera.

                      CONNER
                 (off camera)

      Shit.

5. EXT. DUSK. CU WRIST WATCH   5.
CU wrist watch. The digital display shows
17.05.

                    CONNER
                 (off camera)
        Shit. Shit.

6. (as shot 3.) EXT. DUSK. MID SHOT   6.
Conner jumps over a rickety fence and dives
through a hedge.

7. EXT. DUSK. REVERSE   7.
Conner comes through the bush and slides down
a bank. He lies still. The car brakes hard and
doors slam.

8. EXT. DUSK. MCU CONNER'S FACE   8.
Conner looks indecisive then looks down at his
watch and takes off along the ditch. A dog
starts barking furiously then yelps in pain.

9. EXT. DUSK. ECU CONNER'S FACE   9.
Conner stops, screws up his face but keeps
going.

10. EXT. DUSK. WIDE SHOT DITCH   10.
Conner runs away from camera. He scrambles up
onto the road and heads towards town.

<u>11. EXT. DUSK. THE SKY IS DARKER. CLOSE TO TOWN. MID-SHOT CONNER RUNNING TOWARDS CAMERA</u>
11.

Conner is running down the road towards camera. Headlights swing around a bend behind him, the car approaching fast. Conner doesn't break step but dives straight into the hedge.

<u>12. POV FROM HEDGE</u>   12.

A black BMW speeds past. There are four men in the car.

<u>13. EXT DUSK. ECU WATCH</u>   13.

CU Conner's watch. Display shows 1710.

> CONNER
> (off camera)

Bastards.

<u>14. EXT. DUSK. THE SKY IS DARKER. MID SHOT FROM INSIDE SMALL BACK YARD</u>
14.

Conner leaps over the fence into the garden. He hesitates, all senses alert.

<u>15. EXT DUSK. MID SHOT REVERSE</u>   15.

A dark terraced house. The washing line holds a row of shirts.

> CONNER
> (off camera)

That's handy 'arry.

Conner walks into scene, strips off his torn tee shirt and grabs a shirt. A light comes on in the house.

<u>16. EXT. DUSK. MID SHOT ALLEY   16.</u>
Conner leaps over wall into shot. He puts on the shirt then looks up.

<u>17. POV DOWN ALLEY (CLOSE TO END)   17.</u>
A kid stands astride a mountain bike watching Conner.

<u>18.(as shot 16)EXT. DUSK. MID SHOT ALLEY   18.</u>
Conner puts a finger to his lips.

<u>19. (as shot 17) POV DOWN ALLEY   19.</u>
The kid takes off

<u>20. EXT. DUSK. MID SHOT DOWN STREET FROM</u>
<u>ALLEY   20.</u>
CAMERA FOLLOWS ACTION
The kid is riding as fast as he can. Conner comes into scene and watches as the kid stops at a house and bangs on the door. The door opens and a man looks out. The kid points back towards Conner who ducks back in the alley. The man ducks back into his house.

                    CONNER
                (back to camera)
        Bollocks.

Conner dashes across the street to the
corresponding alley on the other side from where
he came. The kid shouts into the house.

                     KID
                (fifty yards away)
        Dad, Dad.

Conner gives him the finger and runs down the
alley. In the distance two men (silhouette)
enter the alley. Conner ducks behind a wheelie
bin. The men get closer then stop by the bin.
Conner freezes.

                    MAN 1
            (Black, Heavy. London accent)
        What you going on about?

                    MAN 2
        (White, Short, Tough. Geordie accent)
        I said, It's not that he's bright man.
        He's a stupid fucker but then again he's
        not that stupid, if you get my drift.

                    MAN 1
        D'you speak fuckin' English round here?

                    MAN 2
        I mean, (speaks slowly) he's not going
        to be at his brother's man.

                        MAN 1
                Yeah… well we're gonna look.

21. EXT. DUSK CU CONNER'S FACE   21.
CU Conner's face as the men walk past. He looks
down at his watch. He is thoughtful for a beat
then exits frame.

22. EXT. DUSK. THE SKY IS DARK BUT THERE IS STILL
SOME LIGHT LEFT. WIDE SHOT ANOTHER STREET. THE
BLACK BMW IS PARKED.   22.
In very long shot Conner turns into street and
just as quickly turns away.

23. INT. CAR. DUSK   23.
Man 1 is fiddling with the radio, Man 2 is
turned around talking about football to the
two men in the back seats. Man 3 is looking
intently at a house on the other side of the
road and Man 4 is rooting about in a hold-all
by his feet. They all miss Conner.

24. EXT. DUSK. CU WATCH   24.
CU Conner's watch. The display shows 1720.

25. EXT. DUSK. WIDE SHOT. ANOTHER BACK FENCE
                                                   25.
Conner creeps in via a gate. Camera follows as
he runs up to the patio windows. He knocks on
the window urgently.

<u>26. EXT. DUSK. MID SHOT PATIO WINDOWS   26.</u>
A thirtyish man (**ADRIAN,** Conner's brother) pulls open the curtains. He is shocked. He hesitates a beat then…

> ADRIAN
> (shouting through window)
> Fuck off Conner.

<u>27. INT DUSK. REVERSE OF 26   27.</u>
Midshot Conner through glass. He grimaces.

> CONNER
> (through glass but trying to whisper)
> Come on Adrian. Come on.

Adrian opens the sliding door.

<u>28. INT. DUSK. MID SHOT   28.</u>
Conner enters and goes to give his brother a hug. Adrian pulls away.

> ADRIAN
> (rough)
> You really fucking done it this time. The fucking Thompson twins are offering money. Somebody turned dad over.

> CONNER
> (concerned)
> Is he alright?

                    ADRIAN
As if you give a fuck….yeah, he's all
right. They pushed him around a bit but
they probably believed him when he said
he'd dib you in if he knew where you were.
He's more worried about the dog. Bastards
kicked his dog. What d'you want anyway?

                    CONNER
                (hard)
Don't give me that bullshit Ada. He's
only five minutes up the road and when did
you last see him. He's an irritable old
fucker and your Nancy can't stand him. He
knows I'd be there for him if it came on
top.

                    ADRIAN
Yeah yeah yeah. What d'you want?

                    CONNER
The last of my stuff and to use your lavy.

                    ADRIAN
Well fucking hurry up. They'll be round
here next.

                    CONNER
                (leaving the room)
They're already here. Relax.

Adrian turns towards the front of the room.

                    CONNER
                (continued)

And stay away from the window for fuck's sake.

29. INT. NIGHT. A DARKENED ROOM   29.

The door opens and Conner is framed in the door. He leaves the door open and enters the room. He doesn't switch on the light. He takes a box from inside a wardrobe and crouches down.

30. INT. NIGHT. DARKENED ROOM   30.

Conner crouches beside the bed, he opens a shoe box and takes out a padded envelope. He takes out a bundle of twenty pound notes (a couple of grand). He flicks through then stuffs them into his jeans pocket. He gets up and gingerly opens a curtain.

31. POV THROUGH CURTAINS   31.

The BMW is still there.

                    CONNER
                 (off screen)
        Hello boys.

32. INT. NIGHT. MID SHOT BATHROOM   32.

Conner carefully lifts the lid of the cistern and takes out a package wrapped in a black bin liner. He wipes his hands and unwraps the package. It's a pistol. Conner stands and pushes the gun into his waistband. He pulls the shirt over it and checks himself in the mirror. He splashes water onto his face and slicks back his hair. He dries himself then grins into the mirror. He checks his watch.

33. INT.NIGHT. ECU WATCH   33.

ECU watch. The display is showing 17.30.

                    CONNER
                  (Off screen)
        Just time I think.

34. INT NIGHT. MID SHOT HALLWAY OF ADRIAN'S HO USE   34.

Adrian is replacing the telephone receiver as Conner appears at the top of the stairs.

                    CONNER
        Who was that?

                    ADRIAN
        Nobody. Wrong number.

                    CONNER
        I didn't hear it ring.

                    ADRIAN
        It rang.

Conner runs down the stairs. The doorbell starts chiming. It is an incongruous tune. Somebody starts banging with a fist. Conner dashes down the stairs and pushes his brother into the lounge.

                    CONNER
                  (angry)
        You fucking bastard. You bastard.

<u>35. INT NIGHT MID SHOT ADRIAN'S LOUNGE   35.</u>
Conner runs through the patio doors. Adrian looks impassive.

> ADRIAN
> You don't give a shit.

Man 1 and 2 appear in the garden. The others are still banging on the front door. Adrian opens the door.

> MAN 2
> Where is he Ade?

Adrian points to the fence.

> ADRIAN
> You just missed him. Twenty seconds, no more.

> MAN 2
> (turning)
> Cheers Ade.

> ADRIAN
> When do I get the money?

> MAN 1
> You don't. Man'll grass his own bruv ain't worth shit.

<u>36. EXT NIGHT. WIDE SHOT ALLEY   36.</u>
Conner is running away from camera as Man 2 climbs over the fence. Man 1 comes out of the gate and runs after Conner.

                    MAN 1
                  (to Man 2)
              What you on? You pratt

37. EXT. NIGHT. WIDE SHOT ROW OF GARAGES   37.
Conner runs around corner and up and past
camera. Man 1 closely followed by Man 2 run
round corner and up and past. A car drives out
of a garage and away leaving garage door open.

38. EXT.NIGHT. WIDE SHOT HIGH STREET.DESERTED   38.
Conner runs into street camera right. Runs
into the middle of the road towards camera
then veers camera left down foot passage. Man
1 and 2 run into street, stop and look around.
Man 1 runs towards camera. Man 2 dials mobile
phone.

39. EXT. NIGHT. WIDE SHOT PASSAGE WAY   39.
Conner runs towards camera in silhouette.
Lights from the high street flare.

40. EXT. NIGHT. WIDE SHOT HIGH STREET   40.
The black BMW screeches to a halt and Man 2
jumps in. Car roars off down high street

41. EXT.NIGHT.WIDE SHOT FACING PASSAGE WAY   41.
Conner races out of passage and pauses. The
backs of the shops have one floor, flat roofed

annexes. Conner uses a drain pipe and gets
onto a roof.

42. EXT.NIGHT.MID SHOT CONNER ON ROOF   42.
Conner lies flat on the roof. He pulls the gun
from his waistband. Man 1 runs from the passage
and stands below Conner.

                    MAN 1

     Bollocks.

Hold shot as BMW screeches to a stop. Man 2
gets out.

                    MAN 2

     Anything?

                    MAN 1

     He could be anywhere. Fuck it. You better
     tell the twins we lost him.

                    MAN 2

     No fucking way man. We say he was gone
     from his brother's when we got there.

                    MAN 1

     Go on then.

43. EXT. NIGHT. STREET LEVEL. LOW ANGLE CAMERA
IS DIRECTED AT THE POINT CONNER IS HIDING   43.
Man 2 dials his mobile. Man 1 lights a cigarette.

MAN 2
Yeah it's Carson...No show....Yeah...No we tried there...Nothing
(becomes ingratiating) Yeah I know Marty but we done that...Yeah I know Marty...but....
(to Man 1, puts phone away) we keep looking.

Man 1 and 2 get back into the car and it drives away. Conner peers over the gutter. Grins.

44. EXT. NIGHT. WIDE SHOT MANSION FLATS. SLOW TRACK IN BELOW STAIRS LEADING TO ENTRANCE   44.
Conner is hiding in the shadows.

45. EXT.NIGHT. ECU WRIST WATCH   45.
CU watch. The display shows 17.40.

46. EXT.NIGHT. WIDE SHOT SIDE OF BUILDING 46.
Conner hoists himself onto the dustbin shed then climbs the drain pipe.

47. EXT.NIGHT. CU DRAIN PIPE FIXING   47.
As Conner climbs by the fixing shifts and comes away from the wall. Conner freezes. The fixing holds. Conner climbs on.

48. EXT.NIGHT. WIDE SHOT FROM THE GROUND 48.
Conner is level with the second storey of the flats. He leans over to a small window.

CONNER

Yes.

Conner pushes open the window and scrambles in. His legs 'wiggle' for a second then he's gone.

49. INT. NIGHT. DARKENED KITCHEN   49.
Conner gets off the draining board. He knocks a saucepan off the side but he catches it. Voices off. Conner creeps to the door, which is slightly ajar and peeks through.

50. INT. NIGHT KITCHEN   50.
CU Conner's face as he peeks through the door. He starts to grin then opens the door.

51. INT. NIGHT. LIT ROOM. WIDE SHOT   51.
A naked couple are in the 'sixty nine' position on a sofa. The man (**PAUL**) jumps up and grabs a wine bottle from a coffee table. The woman (**KATE**) screams then relaxs. She covers herself with a 'throw' and stands.

PAUL
(shouting)
What the fuck?....(Covers himself with a cushion)...For fuck sake Conner...What do you want?

                    CONNER
                    (Hard)
       Shut your gob Paul. Piss off.

                    PAUL
       Oh I'm so scared...not...you piss off, you
       can't walk in here like you own the fucking
       joint...

52. INT. NIGHT. LIT ROOM. CU KATE.   52.

                    KATE
       Just give us a minute Paul. Go in the
       kitchen will you.

53. INT. NIGHT. LIT ROOM. TWO SHOT PAUL AND
CONNER   53.

                    PAUL
                  (petulant)
       I'm not standing in the kitchen bollock
       naked while you two get re-acquainted.
       Tell him to get lost.

Conner picks up Paul's discarded shirt and
trousers and hands them to him.

                    CONNER
       Go in the kitchen or fuck off. Just get
       out of my face.

Paul turns his back and pulls on his trousers.
He walks into the kitchen and slams the door.

54. INT. NIGHT. LIT ROOM. CU CONNER   54.

                    CONNER
          Didn't take you long.

55. INT. NIGHT. LIT ROOM. WIDE SHOT   55.
Kate lights a cigarette.
                    KATE
                  (Shrugs)
          You left.

                    CONNER
          You knew I'd come back.

56. INT. NIGHT. LIT ROOM. CU KATE   56.

                    KATE
          Yeah, for the money.

57. INT. NIGHT. LIT ROOM. CU CONNER   57.

                    CONNER
     (Takes cigarette and has a long drag)
     I came back for you. There is no money.

58. INT. NIGHT LIT ROOM. TWO SHOT   58.

                    KATE
          That's not what I heard

                    CONNER
              (Hands back cigarette)
         You heard wrong

59. INT. NIGHT. LIT ROOM. CU KATE   59.

                    KATE

         What do you want Conner?

                    CONNER
                 (off camera)
         A blow job

Kate cracks up and starts coughing on her
cigarette.

60. INT. NIGHT. LIT ROOM. WIDE SHOT   60.
Conner is laughing.

                    PAUL
              (through kitchen door)
         You all right Kate?

               KATE & CONNER
         Fuck off Paul. (They both laugh)

Paul stalks out of the kitchen and goes
directly to the other door. He glares at Kate
and ignores Conner. He slams the outside door
and they both laugh louder.

                    CONNER
         Why Paul for Christ's sake?

61. INT. NIGHT. LIT ROOM. CU KATE   61.

                    KATE
     He's got money. He doesn't run around or
     disappear for weeks…and he gives great head.

62. INT.NIGHT. LIT ROOM. TWO SHOT   62.

                    CONNER
     I noticed.

                    KATE
                 (good natured)
     How long were you in there you bastard?

Conner looks at his watch.

                    CONNER
     Fuck. I gotta go

Kate lets the 'throw' fall to the floor.

                    CONNER
             (looking at his watch again)
     I could send for you

                    KATE
     Whatever…..they came round here…the
     Thompson boys.

<u>63. INT. NIGHT. LIT ROOM. MCU KATE   63.</u>
She takes another drag of her cigarette. She
is comfortable naked.

                    CONNER
                  (off camera)
      The Thompson's boys or the Thompsons?

                     KATE
      The twins. They'll find you you know.

<u>64. INT. NIGHT. LIT ROOM. WIDE SHOT   64.</u>
Conner pulls her to him and kisses her hard.
He then leaves by the front door.

                    CONNER
                (after the kiss)
      Not where I'm going. I'll call you.

<u>65. INT. NIGHT. LIT FLATS CORRIDOR. WIDE   65.</u>
Conner comes towards camera to stairwell.
Paul is sitting on the stairs looking glum.

                    CONNER
      It's you she wants mate. Just look after
      her will you.

Paul looks up surprised, pleased.

                     PAUL
      I will.

Conner walks down the stairs. Paul gets up and heads back to Kate's flat. He doesn't see Conner grinning.

66. INT.NIGHT MID SHOT DIMLY LIT HALLWAY 66.
Conner is by the door of the mansion flats. He checks outside then looks at his watch.

67. INT. NIGHT. CU WRIST WATCH 67.
CU watch the display shows 17.55.

68. EXT. NIGHT. WIDE SHOT STREET BY MANSION
FLATS 68.
Conner exits flats and looking both ways, heads away from camera. He stops by a car, a silver Escort.

69. EXT. NIGHT. POV SILVER ESCORT 69.
Focus on 'shaking Elvis' on the dash. Camera moves to 'gonk' hanging from rear view mirror.

                    CONNER
                 (off camera)
     You always had good taste Paul. Cheers
     mate.

The passenger window is smashed by a gun.

70. EXT. NIGHT. MID SHOT STREET 70.
Conner scrambles into the Escort from the

passenger side and fiddles about under the dash. The car starts and Conner drives off.

                    CONNER
          (under engine noise. Shouting)
     Yee..Hah.

71. EXT. NIGHT. WIDE SHOT FROM WITHIN CEMETRY LOOKING TOWARDS CLOSED GATES   71.
Seen from within the cemetry the Escort screeches to a halt. Conner jumps out and without hesitation climbs over the gates and as he hits the ground takes off running towards camera. He runs up and past.

72. EXT. NIGHT. POV AT GRAVE   72.
The headstone reads 'Mary Culkin Rest in Peace'

                    CONNER
          (off camera. Warm)
     Hello Mum.

POV camera track two graves to the left. Headstone reads 'William and Mary Sibbons tragically taken together. Rest in Peace together'

                    CONNER
          (off camera. Equally warm)
     Hello Mister and Missus Sibbons.

73. EXT. NIGHT. MID SHOT SIBBONS' GRAVE   73.

Conner kneels and starts to dig with a small shovel he retrieves from beneath a nearby bush.

74. EXT. NIGHT. CU SIBBONS' GRAVE   74.

As the earth is moved a battered ruck sack is revealed. Conner pulls it from the ground and brushes it off. He then replaces the earth and smooths out the plot. He stands and pauses a while.

>   CONNER
>   (off camera)
>   Sorry about that....thanks for looking
>   after it.

Conner turns and exits frame.

75. EXT. NIGHT. WIDE SHOT STREET OUTSIDE CEMETRY   75.

The Escort roars off. In long shot the car brakes hard and swings left into the high street.

76. EXT. NIGHT. CONNER'S POV DRIVING   76.

The BMW is coming towards camera.

>   CONNER
>   (off camera)
>   Whoops…

<u>77.INT.CAR.NIGHT. MIDSHOT FROM BACK SEAT   77.</u>
Conner ducks down onto the passenger seat.

<u>78. INT. BMW CAR. NIGHT. MIDSHOT FROM BACK
SEAT   78.</u>
The 'driverless' Escort passes. The men all
look.

                    DRIVER
     A...look at that...

                    MAN 1
     Turn round...quick.

<u>79. INT.CAR.NIGHT. CU REAR VIEW MIRROR   79.</u>
CU rear view mirror. The BMW does a screeching
U-turn.

                    CONNER
                 (off camera)
        Shit.

<u>80. EXT. NIGHT WIDE SHOT HIGH STREET   80.</u>
The Escort accelerates hard out of shot. The
BMW speeds after it.

<u>81. EXT. NIGHT. MID SHOT SIDE STREET   81.</u>
The Escort swings out of high street and speeds
up and past. BMW screeches to a stop in high
street then has to reverse to make turn. Drives
up and past at speed.

82. EXT. NIGHT. WIDE SHOT GARAGES FROM SHOT 35   82.

The Escort screeches into the shot and in one movement swings into the open garage. Hold shot for beat as BMW roars past the top of the street. Hold shot as Escort drives slowly from the garage and turns in the opposite direction from that taken by the BMW.

83. INT. CAR. NIGHT. CONNER'S POV   83.

Camera focuses on road sign indicating 'ferry port'. Car follows directions.

84. EXT. NIGHT. WIDE SHOT OF ROAD LEADING TO DOCKS   84.

The escort is driving away from camera towards an incline. The lights from the docks illuminate the sky. As the car approaches the crest of the incline a boy on a bike rides across in silhouette. The Escort brakes hard.

                         SFX

    Loud bang.

Hold shot. Nothing happens. Then the driver's door opens and Conner falls out onto the road.

85. EXT. NIGHT. MID OVERHEAD SHOT OF CONNER LYING IN THE ROAD   85.

Conner's upper thigh is pumping blood. He pulls the gun out of his waist band and stares at it.

86. EXT. NIGHT. LOW ANGLE CONNER'S POV   86.

The kid from the early scenes comes into frame standing astride his bike. He stares blankly at Conner.

87. EXT. NIGHT. KID'S POV   87.

                    CONNER
                   (quietly)
        Shot meself.

Conner dies.

88. EXT. NIGHT. MID SHOT. CAR. CONNER. BOY ON BIKE   88.

The boy turns to the car and looks in. Still astride his bike he reaches in and pulls out the rucksack. He shoulders the bag and takes off.

89. EXT. NIGHT. WIDE SHOT AS SCENE 80   89.

The boy rides away fast back in the direction he came from. Conner's body lies by the car. Fade to black.

END.

Making Up For Lost Time
- Tracey Regan

Sammy hesitated as she approached the grand oak doors that led to the den and opened them cautiously. She knew, no matter what happened, today would probably be the most emotional day of her life so far.

It had been many years since she was last there but it was just as she remembered. The ancient books that filled the shelves to two walls of the room were in no particular order, as if each one of them might have been read just yesterday. There was one chair, and next to it a small occasional table, with half a cigar extinguished in an ashtray and a knobbly well-used walking stick leaning against it. The sumptuous worn-out chair was much smaller than she remembered from her childhood, but still she couldn't tell if there was anyone sitting there. It was placed exactly in the centre of the room, facing the amazing view of the gardens through the elegantly over-sized French doors. Her favourite tree, standing tall and strong, in the centre of the lawn where she had played and daydreamed as a child, seemed to nod a welcome in her direction.

The odious mixture of cigar smoke and cologne filled the air, yet the fire crackled a welcome she hadn't expected. She wandered over to the magnificent marble mantle and was surprised to see a large recent picture of herself, alongside a selection of other family photos. She studied each one carefully, stopping to pick up a picture that brought a tear to her eye. It had been taken in that very room. A blue-eyed toddler, with a smile to warm the coldest day was opening her arms for a cuddle.

"That's my favourite too." The unexpected voice startled Sammy and she jumped nervously almost dropping the picture. The voice was broken and frail and not familiar to her at all. "I wasn't sure you would come," stammered her grandfather. As she turned, her gasp was audible. Had she been eight years old, as she was the last time she saw him, she would have run and jumped into his strong arms, and his 6ft tall frame would have lifted her high in the air, his booming laugh comforting and loving. Now, as he unsteadily rose to his feet, she barely recognised him. She rushed to his side and wrapped her arms gently around him, enveloping his tiny frame with her own.

"Hello Poppa," she choked. Unable to find suitable words for the moment, they just held each other for what seemed an eternity. As Sammy helped him back into his chair, she sat at his feet holding his hand, and tears began to stream down her face.

This wasn't the reaction she had expected of herself. On the long flight from Australia to England, she had stoically promised that she would give her grandfather a piece of her mind. Whatever his reason for wanting to see her, after all these years, she was angry. Why now? Why had he not contacted her for so long? She had adored him when she was a child, and she was pretty sure he had adored her too, but when her father had moved out, it seemed as if she no longer existed. Her grandfather interrupted her thoughts. "Do you remember this room, Samantha?" She looked up, with a smile.

"I do Poppa. It's pretty much all I remember of my childhood." She could remember sitting next to the big old chair, just as she was now, with a colouring book, the French doors wide open on a beautiful summer's day, and the sweet smell of a cake cooking in the kitchen. "Is Gracie still working for you?"

"Sadly no. She was a lot older than she looked and passed on several years ago. She was like family to me and I miss her dearly." Sammy's face hardened. How could he talk of family when she hadn't seen or heard from him for 15 years? When she'd arrived in Australia all those years ago, she'd written letter after letter. She'd even made up crazy stories, convincing herself her grandfather must have died in a car crash or had a terrible accident, or surely he would be in contact. She could never quite believe that he had just forgotten her. And then last week, a courier arrived at her house with a plane ticket and a note saying "please come". Sammy couldn't stop the tears.

"Did you really just forget about me?" she asked.

"Oh Sammy, you couldn't possibly think I could forget you," he sighed. "I was sending you letters every month, but I guess you didn't get them." He reached under his chair and pulled out a tattered and worn, huge leather bound photo album. Sammy began looking through it with him. The album was filled with photos, notes and mementos of her life. "I was even there for your dancing show, three years in a row. You never knew...."

He hesitated not able to find the words to tell her it had all started because he and her father had fallen out. It all seemed so ridiculous now. He remembered the day they left. He had refused to pay yet another gambling debt and they'd had a huge fight. He had made the decision not to bail his son out anymore and once a decision was made there had been no swaying him. He just couldn't see any other way. His son's life would never have changed if he'd just kept giving him money. He chose each word carefully. "Well, it's a long story for today, but your Dad was in trouble with some dangerous people. He had to leave the country and I didn't stop him or help him. I guess at the time he couldn't forgive me for that. To be honest, I focused on work after his mum died. I gave him too much money and not enough love. I really wasn't a very good father."

"But you were an amazing grandfather," she smiled up at him, her misty blue eyes melting his heart, "I always felt like you loved me Poppa, even when I never heard from you."

They sat quietly, both deep in their own thoughts. Sammy wanted to be angry, but her love for her grandfather was just too important in that moment. She held his hand and knew that the past couldn't be changed. She could only look forward to the future. Of course her Dad had always loved her but somehow this connection seemed so much stronger. She still had lots of questions and she was sure the emotional roller coaster she was on wasn't going to end today, but she could feel his love for her and she felt as if everything was going to work out.

Her grandfather couldn't contain his guilt any longer. "I did a terrible thing, Sammy. I have to tell you about your mother," he blurted out, with tears in his eyes. "I didn't want your mother in our family. She was only 17 and I thought she'd trapped your father because of who he was and what we had. I paid her off. I paid her a lot of money, and she agreed to walk away and never try to contact you. I'm so sorry." Sammy joined him in the chair and they held each other for a long time. The emotional intensity of the day was beginning to take its toll. She didn't want to leave his side, but she was beginning to feel completely overwhelmed.

"I tracked her down Sammy," he continued, "your mother. She really wants to meet you. Do you think you're up to it? I thought she might be able to come here for dinner sometime soon. When you've recovered from your jetlag."

Of all the things she had prepared herself for before today, this was not one of them and she felt her heart harden, just a little. "I often think about my mother and what she'd be like?" she smiled. "Dad just shuts me down every time I ask a question about her too. We can only do it here. Right here in this room. It's the only place I feel truly safe."

"Of course, my darling," he said as he held her tight, "There is one other thing." He hesitated for just a moment. "I was actually hoping you might want to stay for longer than just a holiday. Would you like to live here for a while? I'd love to get to know you better."

"Oh Poppa, really? I'd love to spend some time with you." Sammy was lost for words. She wasn't just exhausted from the journey she'd made, or the revelations of the day, but the enormity of how her life was about to change was suddenly apparent. She looked out through the over-sized French doors and imagined herself daydreaming under her favourite tree once again. If she played it right, she would never have to work as a waitress in some horrid cafe ever again. And she might get that Jimmy Choo bag she'd been longing for all these years. "Poppa," she said carefully, "If I'm going to be staying with you for a while, do you think we might be able to do a bit of shopping tomorrow?"

"Of course, my darling," said her grandfather, "whatever you need, just ask."

Sammy smiled and held his hand tightly. "It really is good to see you," she said with those misty blue eyes, staring intently into his.

Bush Tragedy
- Tracey Regan

The morning sun sends rays of red and orange searing through thick, thunderous clouds, just like a reflection of yesterday. But then, those clouds had been great spirals of smoke like a twister sweeping across the countryside. Yesterday, the red and orange flames had built an impenetrable wall of heat; it seems amazing now that we were able to get it under control. I breathe deeply and the damp stale ash leaves a dusty taste in my mouth. I can feel my heart beat out of rhythm as my eyes stretch across the desolate, black hillside, empty now of everything but a lonely bird furiously pecking for its breakfast, but finding nothing in the charred, dehydrated earth. My stare falls reluctantly to the remnants of my family home, and my body tightens as Chloe slips her arms tightly around my chest and nestles into the back of my neck, whispering reassuringly.

"It's gonna be ok Jon, we'll get through this. At least we're all safe. I'm just so glad you and the guys managed to stop the fire from spreading around the district. Thank God it's really only our property that's been affected."

All that's left of the house is a mangled heap of twisted iron, as if it's been put through the spin cycle of a giant washing machine.

"I'm alright Chloe," I lie, "...it's just a house."

We stand silently, uncomfortable, watching as a kangaroo hops across the field, clouds of black soot pluming into the air. Yesterday, that field had been a blanket of bright yellow canola. The sound of a distant engine breaks our thoughts. I glance quickly at Chloe, as I recognise the car through the dust cloud snaking up the long, winding driveway.

"Mum!" I try to hug her as my mother pushes me out of the way and rushes over to what is left of the house. I can't say I'm surprised at the wail that emits from my mother's enormous chest. Of course, she has every right to show her emotion. The house has been her home for nearly 50 years. I take in deep gulps of air as I realise everything she has to remind her of Dad is gone.

"How could you let this happen Jonathan? I thought you were some kind of hot-shot 'firie'. You've been volunteering for years and you couldn't even stop a little fire before it got out of control. Where are we supposed to live now? Don't think I'm going to stay in that disgusting motel for very long. What are you going to do now? Ever since your dad died the farm's gone from bad to worse. I thought your father was a loser but you seem to be making it a family tradition." She pauses briefly, staring at the bleak, black fields surrounding us.

" …. Oh for goodness sake, give me your phone. Someone needs to do something quickly and as always I can't rely on you, can I?   I'll get on to the insurance people and start organising the local newspaper for a fundraiser."

"..but it's only 6.30," says Chloe gripping tightly on my hand. "We can't start ringing people now………"

"…nonsense. Where's the phone?"

As I wander over to the house and kick around in the wreckage, Mum continues with her tirade. It's always been the same. As usual I just have to walk away and block out everything she says. She's always putting me down. I've never been quite good enough. Poor dad had it too. Always a "loser." Despite what my mother thinks, I don't see my life like that. I've always been part of the community, and I've even started thinking about running for the local council. I was always good at sport as a kid, and train the local Under 13's footy. I've been a volunteer fire fighter too for as long as I can remember.

The sound of a distant motor and tell-tale clouds of dust are snaking along the only road that can be seen from the property out to the horizon. As I look at my watch, I realise I must have been day-dreaming for quite some time. It's 8.30 now and the air around us is beginning to heat up.

Chloe and I walk over to meet Sergeant Tyler as his 4wd pulls up into the driveway that just yesterday was at the front of the house.

"Hey Bob … I wasn't expecting to see you out here so soon." My eyes don't meet his and my voice trails away as I greet my old friend.

"I thought I'd come over and see how you were doing" says Bob, giving me a big, supportive hug. "The boys in town were talking about it this morning but I didn't realise it was this bad out here. How are you holding up?"

"Well, it's obviously not really sunk in yet…" says Chloe coldly "but I guess when you live on the land like we do, well, you never know what might happen. Jon's mum has taken over. She's calling the insurance company."

"There'll be an investigation of course," says Bob. "I'll have to get statements from you all. We can do that later if you like. What happened anyway? Do you know how it started?"

"Well, I was out in the tractor when I first saw the smoke," I sigh.

"It was me who raised the alarm," Chloe interrupts, "…I was half way into town, going to meet the girls for playgroup, when I realised I'd left Jaxon's nappy bag on the kitchen table. Well, of course,

I had to turn back to get it, and that's when I saw the smoke. It was only just visible then, but by the time I'd gotten back up the drive, it was pretty well blazing. I had to come all the way back before I could phone anyone, of course the mobile doesn't work out on the drive. Anyway, it was so lucky I turned back, as Jon's mum was fast asleep in the house. She must have taken a valium or something. It took me ages to wake her up and, well, you can see there's nothing left of the house. I can't imagine what might have happened."

Chloe snuggles into my chest, tears welling in her eyes once again. "I was able to get Jon on the two-way once I'd called the emergency services, and he told me to get mum and the baby out as quickly as possible. He stayed on, of course, to help fight the fire."

"Yeah, I was all the way down near Mason's field. Took me ages to get back here." I add.

Mum bustles over, as I'm sure she doesn't want to miss out on any of the conversation.

"Ah, Mrs. Hepburn," says Bob respectfully. Mum's eyes are soft and wet behind her enormous tortoise-shell glasses, "such a terrible tragedy. Is there anything I can do to assist you?"

"Well, actually Sergeant Tyler, I wonder if you might have a word with your mother at the nursing home where she works. They've been offering me a room there for quite some time. I know I can't just walk in anytime I like, but, well, it can't hurt to get the ball rolling so to speak. And I've got nowhere to live now," she gives me a long, lingering look. "Jonathan and Chloe have enough to worry about without me."

"Ok," Bob smiles sympathetically, "I'll make some enquiries as soon as I get back into town." I breathe out loudly as he turns to his car. "Oh, forgot to tell you, the fire inspector has called already and said he'd come and have a quick look this morning." As he pulls out down the drive ash sprays high into the air, like a mini-mushroom cloud. Chloe is holding me tight like she doesn't want to let me go. I want to push her away but know it will upset her.

"Why don't you go back to your mum's for a while?" I say gently. "There's nothing we can do here right now. I'm sure Jaxon is missing you. He needs you. He can probably sense there's something wrong. If you take my mum and her car back to town, I'll come in your car later. I'll just stay here until the fire inspector's done, I'm sure it won't be too long."

"I hope you're not making decisions for me again Jonathan?" Mum interrupts

"Well, maybe you should head back into town, there's nothing you can do here. You can have some breakfast, and a nice cup of tea, and then go see if they've got a room for you at the nursing home. It does seem to be a good option for you right now." Mum looks doubtful but I'm pretty sure the idea of a nice cup of tea sways her.

"Ok Jonathon. I will head back to town. As you say there's nothing we can do here and it is all rather depressing. Don't hang around too long. There's plenty to be done and organised and I will need your help. Jonathon. Are you listening?"

"Yes Mum, I won't be long. I do have to wait for the fire inspector though," I trail off as I notice Chloe glaring at Mum. I'm surprised the two of them aren't arguing as normal. The women in my life really do make things difficult. I can't wait for them to leave. I wonder hesitantly if Chloe knows that I know what she's done. As I catch her eye, I'm guessing she does, as I can see a brief flash of fear behind her eyes.

As they leave, I look nervously at my watch and wonder if I'm doing the right thing letting Chloe and Mum drive the 30 minutes into town together, especially after what's happened. I rush around to the rear of what is left of the barn where the fire started and I can't believe Chloe could have been so stupid. With my experience and knowledge in bush fires I knew very quickly this morning what had caused the fire. Chloe has been angry for a long time about the way mum treats me, but I can't believe she's gone this far. I can only be thankful that she must have had a twinge of guilt because at least she did get mum out of the house. But now I have no idea how to feel about Chloe and our last 10 years together, knowing what she's capable of. I manage to clean up all traces of the accelerant that started the fire and try and make it look like the tree near the power lines must have caused it. I had only trimmed it back a few months ago but it's the best I can do at short notice. I realise by tampering with the evidence, I could leave myself open to accusation. But what can I do?

As the tell-tale sign of a vehicle snakes up the driveway, my hands start to shake. The ordeal of the last 24 hours has kicked in. I hope I can compose myself for long enough to convince the inspector that it was nothing more than a terrible 'natural' bush fire. Only time will tell.

Snakes & Ladders
- Kelly Van Nelson

Miranda clapped hard as the ball soared through the air and dropped through the metal hoop. She hovered on the sidelines next to Suzy, who was shivering in a purple netball dress made of breathable, micromesh fabric that was too tight for her plump body. Even in the northern suburbs of Western Australia, when it should be warm, the Spring weather was occasionally unpredictable. This morning, after a bowl of her favourite cereal, Miranda had used voice command to ask her new smart phone about the Perth forecast. That Siri woman had answered back that the day would be sunny, but she was wrong.

There was a bite in the air and a strong breeze was starting to toss leaves down from the trees growing along the far side of the netball court. They were a distraction from play, floating around like green confetti at a wedding. Miranda was glad she'd suspected the smart phone was not as smart as her. She'd been clever enough to bring a jumper along, otherwise she would be shivering like everybody else.

"Go, Collette," Suzy shouted at the pretty redhead who was team Captain. Miranda loved Collette, who was an outstanding player, but she hated Suzy's high-pitched voice. Suzy sounded like she'd sucked the helium from enough balloons to decorate an eleventh birthday party for every single girl on the Stormtroopers team.

Miranda did the right thing and tried to think nice thoughts about Suzy, but nothing came to mind. She was just plain irritating. The way she played with her hair whenever she was substituted, sucking on the end of her stupid inside-out yolk braids. Her prim and perfect mother must spend ages weaving them for her every Saturday morning. And the way she always dragged her left foot when the ball was in her hands. Suzy was a dummy. Everyone else on the team had mastered the basic rule about no stepping with the ball.

"Coach, when can I go back on to play?" Suzy whined from behind the yellow line.

Coach Becky ignored her as she jogged around the perimeter of the court.

"Come on, girls. Tighter. Keep it tighter. You're giving them way too much space."

Miranda thought Coach Becky should wear army camouflage when she was barking orders at the troops. Even the subs in the trenches were caught up in her commands, waiting to be called upon to fire on the enemy. Coach Becky didn't even let anyone take a toilet break. The enemy was quick off the mark, their lanky Wing Defence player intercepting a perfectly decent lob from Collette. The opposition snatched the advantage, covering the length of the court in a flash to take a goal. Miranda groaned.

"What's the score now, Suzy? It must be close." Suzy shrugged so Miranda narrowed her green eyes. "Well, go and ask."

"I can't move. I hurt my foot during that last quarter."

"When?"

"As I jumped to get that tip to stop them smashing us. That's why Coach Becky took me off."

"No, it's not. It was just your turn to sit out." Miranda knew she sounded spiteful, but Suzy needed to toughen up. "Why do you bother playing when every little knock makes you cry?"

Suzy's mouth started to quiver. Miranda noticed it was also turning blue from the wind. Her lips were wobbling like that tasty blue jelly served at Collette's party last month. Best party ever. The jelly had made every kid in year six resemble an epic Smurf. Suzy rubbed her foot.

"Coach Becky saw me twist my ankle."

Miranda rolled her eyes. "Whatever."

Two spectating mothers were gorging on their second round of takeaway coffees bought from the refreshment van parked beside the umpire's office. They were sitting on canvas foldable camping chairs a few paces from Miranda and Suzy. In between sipping, they kept putting their cardboard cups in the drink holders built into the arms of their camping chairs. Miranda had never liked the posh witches, with their tartan fleece blankets thrown over their stick insect legs. The half-time whistle blew.

"Oranges time." Suzy jumped to her feet and skipped over to the team who were gathering together in a huddle on one side of the court. Miranda followed with a bounce in her step from her new Air Flex training shoes.

"I thought you said your foot was sore." Suzy turned and stared back silently. Miranda hated her googly eyes that were too big for her ugly pixie face.

"Where are the oranges?" Coach Becky asked. "Who was rostered to bring them?"

Miranda stared in the direction of the posh mothers who had their heads bent in deep conversation. All they ever seemed to gossip about was hairdressing tips or the latest acrylic nail techniques. Even when the team scored, they had a delayed reaction in cheering. Coach Becky wandered over to Suzy's mum and came back with a pack of snake lollies.

"Unfortunately, there is no fresh fruit today, girls, but you all like snakes, right? A hit of sugar might make you play better." Miranda watched Coach Becky open the candy snakes and offer them around the team. Miranda took one last. A green one because all the best red and yellow ones had gone. Then Suzy, who was standing beside her, grabbed a second snake and bit off the tail.

"Greedy," Miranda said loudly. Fascinated, she watched Suzy's jaw stop moving. There was probably still a piece of mushy lolly in her mouth. The untouched snake head was clenched in Suzy's fist.

"You better eat that bit else your hands will get so gooey the netball will stick to you."

"I don't want it." Suzy bowed her soggy braids towards the ground. Miranda gave a tut.

"Did you know that even when you cut off a snake's head, it can still bite?"

Suzy opened her palm and offered the remainder of her snake to Collette.

"Do you want this?"

"Gross." Collette screwed her snub nose, then she looked at Coach Becky. "Why have we not got oranges?"

"Yeah, who else has ever forgotten something so important?" asked Miranda, staring again at the women on the camping chairs. "I mean, last week I brought oranges and watermelon."

"Not me!" the girls shouted one by one. Suzy blushed. "Mum probably didn't realise it was my turn."

"It's your fault we've got horrible snakes, so eat it, podgy," said Miranda.

Suzy lifted the snake head and put it in her mouth. Miranda put her hands on her hips and watched impatiently as she chewed it slowly as a cow might munch on tasteless grass.

"Next time you should tell your Mum to stop worrying so much about buying coffee and to remember to bring oranges."

"Yeah, Suzy, get your priorities right," added Collette, before marching off court as it was her quarter to sit out.

"Ouch," Suzy exclaimed as Miranda walked past too and knocked her.

"Sorry," said Miranda. "It was an accident. You better not be a cry baby over it. Let's just get the bibs swapped."

The team suddenly dived into a scrum, bare arms flying everywhere as they tugged their bibs off. They exchanged them and stuck the new positions onto the Velcro patches on each other's backs.

"Oh, crumbs." Miranda grimaced when she saw Coach Becky pass Collette's Goal Attack bib to Suzy. "There's not much chance of winning this match if we have to rely on her to attack. I hope the team doesn't slide too much further down the ladder."

Coach Becky glared at Miranda, her mouth hanging open wide. For a moment, Miranda thought Coach Becky was going to say something sharp, but she just stood there, catching flies for dinner. The single shrill of the whistle cut through the babbling noise from the girls, passing on a message to them to scatter across the court, like one of those gastro bugs that swept through entire school populations quickly. Thinking of bug infestations made Miranda suddenly think of head lice as Suzy fiddled with her braids.

"I hope you haven't got nits," Miranda shouted to Suzy as the second half of the game began.

"Has Suzy got nits?" Collette called back from the sideline so loudly several players paused in their play. Miranda nodded. Collette screwed up her face. "That's disgusting!"

"Yuk," said a girl from where she stood, poised in her purple dress on the edge of the semi-circle.

"She better not come near me," the feisty player in Centre position said to nobody-in-particular.

The other team scored another goal but the Stormtroopers team didn't seem to care. They were far more interested in the news that Suzy may have head lice, which travelled all the way from Goal Shooter down to Goal Keeper and all the way across to the camping chairs.

"My daughter has not got nits!" Suzy's mum shouted, jumping up so fast her coffee flew from the cup holder and spilled down her turquoise, active-wear leggings. "Who started the nasty rumour that Suzy has got nits?"

Suzy cast a look at Miranda and failed to notice the ball fly towards her from the hands of the Wing Defence on the opposing team. It smacked her in the nose. The umpire blew hard on her whistle to halt play.

"Blood break! We need the sub," shouted Coach Becky. "Collette, that's you. Get ready to come on."

"Who said she has nits?" bellowed Suzy's mum again. Suzy sobbed loudly as blood trickled down her face and dripped onto her netball dress.

"Miranda said it first. Then Collette."

"I did not say Suzy has nits," said Miranda indignantly.

"Neither did I," said Collette.

Suzy's posh mum handed a tissue to Suzy and then came up to Miranda. She was so close Miranda could see her nostrils flare.

"You'd better apologise."

"I will not."

"This is bullying, Miranda" said Suzy's mum.

"Don't be such a drama queen," Miranda retorted. "Oh, and you've got coffee froth on your lip."

A red rash crept up Suzy's mum's neck and her eyes bulged. They were exactly like Suzy's huge eyes, only they were surrounded by longer lashes decorated with clumpy mascara.

"I'm only trying to help," said Miranda.

Suzy dabbed at her nose. "Mum, I really need to sit down."

"What a palaver. Give her another snake and she'll be fine," said Miranda

"This bullying has to stop." Suzy's mum escorted her daughter off court to swop places with Collette. Miranda picked up her clipboard and pen to finish assessing the Stormtroopers.

"Bullying? What a drama queen. No girl would dare bully anyone while I'm president of the netball committee!"

Suzy's mum glared at Collette and then at Miranda.

"I don't care who you are. Your daughter is a bully and I know exactly who the snake is she learned it from."

Miranda put a cross next to Suzy's name on her player evaluation sheet and added a tick next to Collette, her daughter. The whistle blew, but the game was already lost, and the Stormtroopers slipped down the ladder.

The Ultimate Seduction
- Tracey Regan

Allanah happily grabbed Tony's hand as they strolled along The Embankment watching the sunset cast mystical shadows over the elegant buildings of the London skyline. Tony always loved summer in London, when you could escape the tourists of course. He loved to walk along the river, as the sun's setting rays would light up the Thames with a glow that sometimes made it look almost blue.

The late sunset of an English summer meant most of the commuters had left for the suburbs by now, so it was one of the few times of day you could walk along without feeling caught up in a tide of people. Tony thought it was the most romantic of settings and would often bring new girlfriends down to the river to be cast under his spell. He would talk endlessly and charmingly about the amazing history of London and it's buildings. He was an Architect after all. Well, an assistant at an architectural firm just off The Strand. He would take a small bottle of sparkling wine and sit on his favourite bench until the sun had set. Later, after Tony had mesmerised his new friend with his knowledge and unpretentious air, they would wander hand in hand up to Covent Garden and eat at Tony's favourite restaurant. It was the ultimate seduction. The girls, of course, would always fall for the sweet, sensitive way he spoke, and he was always so respectful and attentive. The fact that he had strongly defined features, and thick, black hair falling over his soft hazel eyes couldn't go unnoticed. He looked after himself too. His body was lean and muscular, and he was always well dressed.

Allanah couldn't believe her luck when Tony had introduced

himself at her local sandwich bar a few weeks ago.

"Excuse me. Can I buy you a coffee? I've seen you having lunch here by yourself before and well, you look a little lonely. Do feel like some company?" She'd blushed of course, but was happy for his attention.

"Sure. Sit down. My name's Allanah. I've just started a new job and haven't really had the chance to make many friends yet."

"Tony," he said, pulling out the chair. "So what's your story? Do I detect an Australian accent?"

"Yep. Born and bred in a small town near Perth. My friend and I came travelling straight to London and I've been here for about a month now. It's my first time anywhere really. I haven't even travelled around Aus," she laughed. "It's been so overwhelming, but I'm having a great time and I've got myself a good job," she sighed a little. "You were right about me being a little lonely though. My friend had to make a rush trip home for a family emergency."

"Wow, all alone in a big city. That's pretty brave for a novice traveller."

"Oh it's not so bad. All the Aussie's at the backpacker's are great fun and pretty friendly – it's like an instant family."

They'd had coffee regularly since that day, but tonight was their first real 'date'. As Allanah and Tony sat together on the bench overlooking the river and sipping wine from two plastic glasses, she felt the happiest she'd felt in a long time.

"Thanks for inviting me to dinner Tony, I thought you were never going to ask me on a proper date."

"I don't pick up girls at lunch all the time you know," said Tony with a grin, "I like to get to know people first. I only take really special girls out to dinner." Allanah blushed. She was doing that a lot when Tony was around. She hadn't really had that many boyfriends, and certainly none of them were anything like Tony. She found herself imagining their first kiss. She had to pull herself together. She couldn't fall for the first guy that took her out for dinner could she? She had to take things slowly. This was their first date after all, but she couldn't help being infatuated.

He was so easy to talk to. She had been angry with herself, in the first week they met because she'd basically told him everything about her life. It was like she had to blurt it all out to someone, anyone who was happy to listen. And Tony was very good at listening. She had told him how her parents had died in a car crash a few years ago, and how she felt so alone, basically because she had no family left. She'd been an only child and her family consisted of an old eccentric uncle living in South America who she hadn't seen in 15 years.

Allanah felt a little giddy as they sauntered up to Covent Garden for dinner. She was truly having the best night of her life. The food was delicious, the wine flowed and they laughed and giggled through dessert. She couldn't help but fantasise about the rest of the night.

"Come on," said Tony, "I'll take you home, my car's just around the corner."

"But you can't drive," said Allanah alarmed, "you've had way too much to drink."

"Nonsense!" said Tony laughing, "you're the one who's drunk all the wine tonight, I've been talking far too much to drink anything. Come on. I'll be fine to drive. Where do you live?"

"mmm…it might be a bit far. The backpackers is in Clapham."

"No problem," said Tony, "it's on my way." Allanah hesitated, but only momentarily.

"Ok, take me home," she said with what she thought was an alluring smile.

Allanah struggled to walk the distance to Tony's car. As they reached the Porsche, Allanah stumbled and fell back against the door, pulling Tony to her. His lips gently landed on hers, and she kissed him, hard on the mouth. She giggled and tried to kiss him again, but he pulled back looking startled, even a little conflicted. He laughed it off.

"Let's get you home hey."

As Allanah put on her seat belt, she was already struggling to keep her eyes open. She was so tired.

"I might just have a little snooze, Tony. Wake me when we get to Clapham, and I'll give you direc….", but Allanah had already passed out. Tony gazed at Allanah for a moment and thought how beautiful she was. He really shouldn't think like that. The kiss had clouded his thoughts. He shrugged and concentrated on the road, as a light rain began to make patterns on the windscreen. He left The Strand and headed east, not west, and sung along to the radio before he arrived at his destination; an inconspicuous warehouse in Whitechapel, in London's East End.

Tony flashed an entry card at the monitor and the garage door slowly lifted. He drummed his fingers on the steering wheel, waiting for the door to open. Why was it taking so long? He looked to see if anyone was around but the alley was clear, as usual. Once inside his anxiety faded, as a familiar face approached the car. Still

Tony was always a little nervous in his presence, but then he guessed that everyone was.

"So what have you brought for me tonight Tony? Number three this month hey. You must be feeling rich." Tony was tossed a brown paper bag, bulging with cash. "Are you sure no-one's gonna come looking for her?"

"She's got no family and no real friends here in London – just like usual. I've been doing this for long enough now to know what I'm looking for." He added with a grin, "Have I ever let you down?"

"Not yet, Tony, not yet….." he said, lifting Allanah from the car as if she were a tiny rag doll, her red curly hair almost dragging on the floor .

"Hey come on. Be careful with that one, she's special," said Tony.

"Yeah they all are. See ya again soon hey?"

"I'll be in touch," said Tony and he floored the Porsche as he left the building. He opened the bag with one hand and notes spilled over the floor as he turned the corner and headed for home, singing along to the radio.

What's In It For Me?
- Tracey Regan

I 'm not sure exactly how long it's been since I was last stabbed with a syringe and pumped full of heroin. I do know that not having heroin after spending months with no choice has to be the worst experience of my life. It has woken me up and living my life without it is far worse than the withdrawal.

I don't know when it started or how long it's been. What I do know is one long blur of dirty dark rooms, and a continuous line of strange men, all speaking at me in a language impossible to understand. I don't know whether it's night or day. I don't really care what they do to me. Until now I've just been moved around like a ragdoll from one room to the next.

But a few weeks ago, the heroin stopped. The plump, elegant woman who gives me clean clothes and occasionally pushes me into the shower sat on the edge of the bed and took hold of my hand. "Red" she said, in her slight accent, (I've just discovered that's what they call me, because of my mass of red, curly hair), "some of the high paying customers don't want drug-fucked girls…..and well, we've decided to clean you up….it's gonna be a tough couple of weeks for you, but you'll get through it…..OK?"

It was the first time I remember her talking to me, but she seemed to know me. She even had a look of concern in her eyes. She was right to be concerned. Suddenly I was awake, and aware.

The large decaying room, with paint stripping from the walls had 4 single beds in each corner, and nothing else except a huge old radiator that pumped out sweltering heat. A doorway to a squalid room with a toilet and basin, emitted a smell that encouraged wretching from the moment I woke. There was one tiny window up high in the far corner of the room, but the bulb that hung from the centre sent out an eerie light 24 hours of the day. No-one thought to turn it off. On each bed, was a girl I assumed was just like me. And that was scary. They seemed so tiny even the sallow skin that sat on their bones looked like it was a size too big. Their hollow eyes, like looking into a pool of stagnant water, were so black and lifeless that nothing could survive in their depths. We didn't dare have feelings for fear of the madness that would ensue. There were no words spoken.   We were just too aware for the first time of the incredible situation we were in. As soon as my keeper left, I had leapt from my bed to try and escape the room, but there wasn't even a handle on the inside of the door.

After a few days of horrific withdrawal symptoms, hot and cold fever, shakes, cramps and vomiting, apparently it was time to 'get back to work'. I had a cold shower for the first time in days, and dressed, if you can call it that, in some clean lingerie. She took me past the kitchen where two girls looked up and stared with pity in their eyes. The smell of bacon cooking made my insides ache.

I knew what she expected from me, but it was a completely new experience now that I wasn't drugged beyond all memory and feeling. I was shoved into a room that looked like a scene from a 70's porno. There was a four-poster bed with silky material hanging from the beams. A dull red lit the room just enough to make it look acceptable, but the sight of whips and handcuffs hanging from various hooks on the walls made my empty stomach churn.

I remember gasping as he walked into the room. The man

who was to take all I had left. His huge hairy frame stumbled as the door burst open. I will never forget the smell of whisky, smoke and sweat as his crushing weight pounded against my tiny body, but all other thoughts and feelings I have blanked out.

So here I am, a few weeks on, stronger and healthier than I was that day. Ready to put my plan into action. I decided that I would bide my time, play the good girl and gain the trust of my captors to plan my escape, but I can't take it any longer and know I have to try and make a run for it, before I become a walking robot with no thought or feeling left.

It won't be easy. I have no idea what awaits me outside of the building that has held me captive. I've managed to collect a few clothes even though we're not supposed to have anything but what we're wearing. I'm also in a room on my own right now, so. I've been able to wander around and get a good look at the place at different times of day. I've been so cooperative that no-one watches me too closely these days. Well, at least that's what I tell myself.

I have talked to no-one of my plans as I just don't know who to trust. Most of the girls are so totally out of it that speaking is pointless. As for the few girls like me who are no longer drugged, no conversation seems to be the unspoken rule. Even if we spoke the same language, to talk about our situation would definitely not help our mental state; it all feels so helpless. But I am allowed to watch some TV now so I'm beginning to pick up a few words. Maybe that will help me when I get outside.

So yesterday a 'customer' hit me so hard across the face that they've told me I'm not required for a few days. I'm thinking it's the best opportunity I've had to try and escape.

I know that the quiet time in the house is between 5 and 6am. They've only got one man on the door around then. Well the only door I know of. There's a lounge area and everyone enters and leaves through that one door. I've searched around as much as I can and that door is the only way I can see anyone at all going in or out. I've managed to steal a syringe, and i'm just going to rush at the doorman and stab him straight in the eye with it before I open the door and step through. I won't feel bad. Every one of those doormen have done bad things to me in the past few weeks.

The worst of it is just not knowing what I will face if I get through the door. I'm hoping for a deserted alley, leading to a main street of a busy city, where I can find a policeman or anyone that can take me as far away from the building as possible. My worst nightmare would be to walk straight into another room, full of my 'captors' all playing cards, counting money and still drinking whisky.

As I lie on my bed, it's 11.45pm and scenario's rush through my head with all possible outcomes of what I intend to do. Can I really summon up every last piece of courage I have left to go through with my plan? I can tell myself my prison is not so bad. I get to watch TV and eat food in my spare time. Maybe I could live the next 5 years of my life like this, before I look too old or get some terrible STD, though I've probably got that already. They're only going to take me out and throw me in a ditch when I'm no use. I'd rather be in a ditch right now than wait 5 years for the inevitable after being used and abused for all that time. What's the worse that can happen? They kill me now or put me back on heroin. Both of those options seem pretty good to me. Better than what I've had to endure these past few weeks without drugs.

The five hours I have to lie here, is the slowest most agonising wait of my life. My life plays out like a slow motion silent movie, but it seems most of my memories have been washed away by a tide of heroin, or maybe it's just my own protection mechanism making me forget everything of value.

Finally, it's time. The house is quiet. My legs are shaking uncontrollably as I put on my tracksuit pants and T-shirt, and stuff the few things I have managed to collect into my pockets. I can barely catch my breath and my heart is beating so hard I'm sure it can be heard over the quiet of the house. I open the door just slightly and check out the hallway. I've done this part before many times with no consequence. Why should it be different today?

With renewed confidence, I quickly move through the house, down the stairs and stop just out of sight of the doorman, who is standing, arms crossed, eyes blinking, somewhere between dozing and wakefulness. The syringe feels tiny and slippery as I clench it in my hand. I hear the shuffling of footsteps on the stairs, and know I can't back out now. My legs are shaking again, as I run at full speed, syringe held high ready to strike. He is certainly taken by surprise, as I lunge with all my strength and hit my target. His hands immediately go to his face, his high-pitched scream alerting the whole house. I can already hear the sounds of sleepy footsteps and doors opening behind me.

The door is harder to open than I had hoped. Three bolts to be undone. The doorman makes a grab for me, but I manage to kick free and get through the door. I hesitate, but just for a millisecond. I so hope it's an empty alley!

It feels like an eternity as the stares of around ten men, all turn to me and the commotion that is unfolding behind me. There is another door just 10 metres away. I have to try and reach that door. I can't give up now.

My legs don't want to work, but i'm making it. Only 5 metres to go, I hear a voice shout, "STOP HER". I know that because of my TV language lessons. I can see everyone is shouting, but suddenly I can't hear a thing. I am down on the floor, and being dragged across the room.

As I'm lifted up, I'm not going without a fight. I spit in his face, and bite the arm closest to me. My spindly legs flail around contacting anything in reach.

Suddenly, my five senses are heightened beyond all memory. I can feel the cold of a steel cylinder pressed tightly to my temple, but I feel no pain. I can hear the piercing screams and shouts of each individual in the room, but not the sound of the explosion, right next to my ear. I can taste the iron rust of my blood as it drips on to my tongue. I can smell that intense smell of whisky, smoke and sweat for the very last time. I can see the grin on my murderers face, but my eyes go to the skylight high above, where beautiful clouds make swirling patterns in the clear blue sky.

It's the first time I have seen sky in a very long time, and I am happy. The wind rushes past my body and I feel like I am flying high, soaring with the birds. I look down and can see an amazing landscape, beautiful green fields, rugged mountains, endless sky.

I am free.

Break Down
- Tracey Regan

The air is crisp and clean, and the distant light of dawn lights the sky, as I stand at the cliff top looking out at the dark of the ocean below. Despite my lack of sleep, I feel ready for the day ahead. I guess there's something about the dawn that clears my clouded, sleepless mind.

I can't believe I left it until the last possible moment on the eve of my sister's wedding to travel the 7 hour drive up the coast. If only I'd left earlier, my car might have broken down in daylight and I may have been able to flag a lift, on this isolated stretch of road. Instead, when I broke down at midnight, with no signal on my phone, I foolishly opted to try and sleep in the car. I had promised my sister I would be there for her wedding breakfast, but I guess she's used to her big brother breaking promises.

I wander up the road, waving my mobile high in the air. Around the bend, I can see a magnificent tree, abundant with leaves, and certainly not the type of tree you'd normally see in this sunburnt part of the country. It's in the grounds of a very old house. A white picket fence borders the perfect country cottage, with its immaculate garden of colourful fragrant roses. Approaching the door, I'm surprised by the smell of coffee and bacon at this time of day.

"Hello," I call. A clucking of chickens breaks the silence and as I turn I'm startled by the vision of a very attractive young woman. Maybe it's the morning sunlight lighting up her long blonde hair, but my heart skips a beat, and my mouth gapes open as I stammer a quick, "Hi", before I make a complete fool of myself. I stare for a while. Her shorts are just a little too short, and her tight t-shirt leaves little to the imagination. As her smile lights up her large green eyes I take a sharp intake of breath. This is ridiculous. I have to say something.

"ummm, sorry it's so early, but my car broke down last night and I can't seem to get any reception on my phone."

"Sounds like a terrible night. You can use my phone if you like." Her voice is hypnotising and I am confused and embarrassed to find that I now do have reception on my phone.

"Er. Thanks. I don't suppose you have the number of a local mechanic? Or I guess I could just call my Dad now?" My question lingers in the air between us.

"Pop in to the kitchen. There's a business card on the fridge. I just need to finish feeding the animals and I'll come inside and make you coffee," she stammers a little, a pink blush rising to her cheeks. "I'm Bronwyn."

"Steve." I blush too, and give her my most awkward smile as I head towards the inviting smell of the kitchen.

The quaint little house is homely but very old-fashioned. The hallway has wood panelling half way up the walls, and 'velvet' swirling patterned wallpaper in a dusty green colour. As I enter the kitchen I 'm surprised at how plain it is, with a small wooden table and chairs in the centre of the room and an old range oven with a bubbling coffee pot on top. The retro fridge has a few business cards stuck to it, and I struggle to pull off the local mechanics, as I wander over to the window to gaze at the beautiful remote landscape.

As I turn, Bronwyn takes me by surprise. She is right there beside me staring out into the distance. I didn't hear her footsteps on the old wooden floorboards.

"It's beautiful isn't it?" she whispers. The hair on my neck tingles. "Sit down, and I'll fetch you some coffee, I bet I know how you take it," she giggles infectiously, "black and two sugars right?"

"How did you know that?" I tease, because I don't have the heart to tell her I like it with lots of milk.

We talk for ages about everything and nothing. I barely even hear my phone as it jumps me back to reality. It's my sister. It's 9am already. My sister's wedding! What the hell am I doing? I answer my phone, with a slightly false smile.

"Susie. Hey, I'm so sorry. My car broke down last night and I'm just about to organise a tow. I think I'm only about an hour away." Susie cuts me off. "Are you ok? You could've called. We've all been worried sick about you. Did you not get any of our messages or calls? …. oh I guess you've just been out of range. Dad's on his way now to get you. Are you on the coast road?"

"Yes. Coast road," I mutter. "I'll head back to the car and wait for him there. So sorry Sis."

"Hey it's not your fault. I'm just glad you're safe."

I hang up and quickly grab Bronwyn's clasped hands on the table. Her eyes holding just a hint of a tear. "I have to go, but I'd really, really like to see you again. I'm staying in town for a few days. I can come by tomorrow maybe."

"Steve. Please don't go now. We've had such a wonderful time."

"I'm sorry I'd love to stay but it's my sister's wedding. And it's not like we won't see each other again. You can make me some strong black coffee tomorrow." I laugh.

"Please don't go. It's so lonely here." Bronwyn whispers harshly, and tears stream down her cheeks.

"Hey come on. Why are you crying? I'll be back tomorrow. I promise." Feeling a little uncomfortable and conflicted about leaving, I give her a hug and a delicate kiss on her soft, inviting lips. "I promise ok."

It takes me 15 minutes to walk back to the car, and I'm shocked to find my dad already there. I rush to give him a hug.

"Jeez Stevie. If only you'd known how close you were to town you could've walked it. It's only about 15 kilometres. You probably would've been in phone range in about 10 minutes. Let's go. We'll sort your car out tomorrow when there's less excitement."

We drive up the road, and I smile as we approach the bend. I wonder if I'll see her in the garden in those 'oh so tight' shorts. But my grin is quickly wiped from my face as we make the turn in the road. I can't quite catch my breath. I am sweating and cold at the same time. My head is pounding and I think I might be going quite mad.

"What is it Steve? Steven. What is it? You look like you've seen a ghost. You've got to breathe mate." Dad is pulling over, but I really don't know what to tell him. The house that I've just visited is there, exactly where I left it not 20 minutes ago, but it certainly doesn't look like the same place. The magnificent tree that had hypnotised me is bare. Half the building is collapsing. The gardens are dead and overgrown. It's obvious that no-one has lived here for a very long time.

"I need to get out and have a look at this place Dad"

"Steve. We've got places to be. Come on."

But I'm already out of the car and running through the front door. The hallway is filled with dead leaves and the green 'velvet' wallpaper is peeling from the dry rot in the walls behind. I don't know what I expect to find, but I don't think Bronwyn will be here tomorrow. Dad's breathless voice and pounding footsteps break my trance.

"What the hell is going on? Are you ok?"

"I will be Dad. Do you know anything about this place? You've lived around here a few years now."

"Not really. You should talk to Jack Owens. He owns all this land. I think it was his grandmother who lived here. She became a recluse when her husband never came back from war. Hey," he grins, "you should meet up with Jack's daughter. Real looker she is. Fabulous green eyes! I'm sure you two would get on well."

"Bronwyn?" I whisper, not meaning to say it out loud.

"Yeah that's right. She was named after his grandmother, I think. How'd you know that?"

"You don't wanna know Dad. You really don't want to know," I sigh as I wander back to the car, questioning everything I've ever believed in, including my sanity.

The Long Man (A Screenplay)
- Ross Cameron

List of Characters   (in order of appearance)

1.	Gerry Thomas	:	Secondary school teacher
2.	Heidi Thomas	:	Amateur sculptor
3.	Peter Middleton	:	Management executive
4.	Mike Williams	:	Corporate video/film producer/director
5.	Sue Williams	:	Former production assistant, amateur sculptor
6.	Rosemary Middleton	:	Former Lawyer, amateur sculptor
7.	Penelope Middleton	:	Daughter (10 going on 20)
8.	Anna-Maria McNamara	:	Child psychologist, amateur painter and sculptor
9.	Helen Cooper	:	IT Consultant, amateur sculptor
10.	Rob Becket	:	Cooper's boyfriend, Australian
11.	Bridget Fairbrother	:	Professional sculptor, healer
12.	Charles Fairbrother	:	Professional artist
13.	Giles Fairbrother	:	Son (18)
14.	Cindy	:	Giles' girlfriend (18)
15.	Hans Muller	:	Anna-Maria's estranged partner, Psychologist
16.	Coach driver		
17.	Old woman		
	Extras	:	Children of group
	Background	:	surfers, car drivers & passengers, Coach passengers

<u>1. EXT. DAY   CARAVAN/CAMP SITE.   OUTSIDE   A
LARGE FRAME TENT.   1.</u>

GERRY THOMAS (early fifties, worn jeans, old
Guernsey jumper, battered 'captain's' hat) is
loading an elderly Mondeo estate. Beach bags,
cold box and windbreak are already stowed. He
carries a bag of charcoal and a barbecue past
his wife HEIDI who sits in shorts and boob tube
facing the sun. GERRY is vaguely irritated.

A new model Land Rover Discovery drives up too
fast and skids to a halt on the grass. GERRY
looks at the damage as if it were his front
lawn.

PETER MIDDLETON (late forties, designer polo
shirt, cargo shorts and Raybans on a granny
string) jumps out of the car.

                    MIDDLETON

  **Hi Gerry, Heidi, I'm just off to get some
  booze. D'you need anything?**

                    GERRY

  **I thought I'd pick something up on the way
  through, why bother going in now when we
  have to go right through later?**

MIDDLETON as he begins to help load the Mondeo
causing GERRY more irritation.

                    MIDDLETON

  **Got to get organised old boy, get ahead of
  the opposition what.**

GERRY

(bemused)

What are you talking about?

MIDDLETON

Taking stuff out of the Mondeo and repositioning
it

**We'll be in convoy won't we….don't want to
be stopping all over the show. We'll get
separated and then what happens? It's Mike's
first time and he doesn't know Constantine.**

GERRY

Putting things back where he had them

**It's only up the road for Christ's sake and
he's got gps, no sweat…..will you please
leave that alone.**

MIDDLETON

Standing back hands raised. Spots GERRY'S
trailer

**Tell you what, why not use your trailer
for everything? We could load everybody's
stuff in that, hitch to the Discovery and
I'll pull it right into the dunes… be just
right.**

GERRY

(Incredulous)

**Are you joking? They don't allow you to drive
on the dunes, it's a bloody conservation**

area. Anyway, the best place is at the far end of the bay, you'd have to drive right along the length of the beach.

MIDDLETON

No worries the old Discovery can cope with it, no problem

GERRY

(More incredulous)

You would wouldn't you….No Peter (speaking as a teacher) we'll go separately and all take what we need. We'll stick to plan A and leave here at seven, be at the beach around seven thirty, set up in the dunes while the kids play and we'll be ready for the sunset at eight thirty.

GERRY slams the back of the Mondeo by way of a full stop and starts to construct a roll up.

MIDDLETON

(Quite cheerful)

Suit yourself Gerry, just trying to make sure everything is tickerty boo

He jumps back into the Land Rover and roars off tearing up more grass.

GERRY

Does he do it deliberately do you think?

HEIDI

Looking up from her book

What dear?

                    GERRY

(Resigned)**Nothing dear.**

2. EXT. DAY   CARAVAN/CAMPSITE.   O U T S I D E
ANOTHER LARGE TENT.   2.

MIKE & SUE WILLIAMS (mid forties) are loading
the boot of an Audi estate.

                    MIKE

**What's happened to the boys? They were
supposed to be helping**

                    SUE

(Good natured)
**Oh they're alright, they're still down
at the beach surfing, Giles and Cindy are
watching out for them. Are we taking our
barby?**

                    MIKE

**Yep we'll take ours. You know what Gerry's
like. It'll take him half an hour to decide
on the right spot. Have you seen Charles and
Bridget's? Can you have an antique barbecue?**

                    SUE

What about wine?

                    MIKE

**We'll stop at the village on the way through
and I'll pick up something for the kids and**

some beers… did you put the jerk spice on the ribs?

SUE

(West Indian accent)

Yeh Man, Yes I.

ROSEMARY MIDDLETON early fifties, enters scene. She wears a long wrap around skirt over a one-piece swimming costume. Her hair is wet and she carries a body board.

ROSEMARY

Hello Sue, Hi Mike, the surf is wonderful; just on the edge of being scary. Are you getting ready for tonight? What are taking?

MIKE

Well I've got some belly pork and some ribs and some chicken thighs and we've smothered it all in the old Jamaican Jerk.

ROSEMARY

Oh, we've only got sausages, our kids won't eat anything spicy. D'you think I should get some steak and some leaves?

SUE

Don't worry Rosemary, he's gone right over the top as usual. We've got enough to feed the five thousand, really, there's plenty.

MIKE

There's this great butchers in Soho Rosey.

It's called Bi-focals or something. You can get anything there, kebabs, ribs, spicy sausos. Its where Dennis gets his stuff for his barby…

SUE starts to load the car and ROSEMARY looks off towards the cliffs.

MIKE

Continues

…. Dennis, he's Michael Caine's agent, he has this huge barby every year. Does all the cooking himself, they're all there, Danial Craig, Idris Elba…last year…

ROSEMARY

Must dash Sue, what are you wearing?

SUE

Shorts and a tee shirt, weather looks great but I'll probably take a cardy or something for later

ROSEMARY

Starting to walking away

Righto, see you about seven

MIKE

Dennis' party was great last year wasn't it love?

SUE

Yeah, smashing babe, where d'you put the

frisby?

The Discovery comes roaring back into the field. ROSEMARY flinches as it slides to a halt outside the Williams' tent. MIDDLETON jumps out, 'drops' the Raybans and approaches the Audi, acknowledging his wife with a pat on the backside in passing.

MIDDLETON

As he walks

Hello love, good time on the beach? Hey Mike, d'you need anything in the village?

MIKE

Well we're going through later aren't we. I'm picking up my booze then and we've got all the food organised.

MIDDLETON

Everybody seems organised except me. I'm supposed to be the management professional around here, I haven't got anything sorted yet.

Laughs and nods head disparagingly.

ROSEMARY (Aside)

Now there's a surprise!

MIDDLETON

(Ignoring ROSEMARY)

I've just been to fill up, you should see the bit of stuff in the garage Mike, gorgeous.

Hell of a rack, you know what I mean.

ROSEMARY walks away and SUE shakes her head and gets on with packing. MIKE frowns at MIDDLETON.

MIDDLETON Continues

Anyway, d'you think I should get a barbeque? They've got a great one in the garage. Double gas burner, lots of gizmos, first class…

MIKE

You don't really need one, we're taking ours, Gerry will definitely take his and Charles has his 1948 version.

MIDDLETON

Its good though. Might get it for back home

ROSEMARY

Walking away not looking back, hard

We have a barbecue at home Peter, <u>you</u> forgot to pack it. We don't need another thing to leave behind.

A young girl (10) PENELOPE MIDDLETON approaches and stops her mother.

PENELOPE

I'm hungry mummy

ROSEMARY hugs the child.

ROSEMARY

**We'll be eating later darling, we're going
to Constantine beach to watch the sunset
and we're having a barbecue**

PENELOPE

Yuk, barbecue. Gross, all that burned meat.

ROSEMARY

stooping down

**There'll be salad darling and cheese, I'll
get daddy to buy some houmus and the sunset
will be beautiful tonight.**

PENELOPE

**Well I don't know, I think I should have
some crisps now in case I can't eat later.
Will there be ice cream?**

The others have all paused watching the
encounter between mother and daughter.

MIKE

We're leaving at seven Rosemary.

SUE

Offering an apple to the child who looks at her
with a sulk

What about an apple Penny?

MIDDLETON

Leaping into the Land Rover. Speaks like the

Terminator

I'll be back.

The car roars off. ROSEMARY and daughter walk away. SUE is left with her apple still offered. GERRY THOMAS enters scene looking after the Land Rover. He's smoking the roll up.

                    GERRY

He's driven to the village three times today. Is Anna-Maria planning to join us do you know?

                    MIKE

Who knows… Hans definitely is, he'll probably be feeding the kids, Anna-Maria will be too busy communing with the universe.

                    GERRY

Irritable

Bloody woman. My year nines have more idea but she genuinely believes she has talent.

                    MIKE

I know, she does my head in. This morning we're eating breakfast out here when little Peony wonders by. I say "Hi Peony, have you had your breakfast?" The kid says "No, I don't know where mummy is." Silly moo has gone off leaving an eight year old alone while she paints another rock. Drives me nuts.

                    SUE

Now, now boys…

                    MIKE

I'm sorry love but it's just not on….

                    GERRY

Heads up!

ANNA-MARIE McNAMARA appears. She is wearing
a long smock over a floor length Laura Ashley
high necked dress. She has a huge floppy straw
hat and a satchel with her paints. She carries
her easel and a larch bunch of ripe barley.

                  ANNA-MARIE

**Sue, Mike….Gerry, I wish you could have been
with me at dawn. I walked beyond the cove
and found an outcrop I hadn't seen before
exposed by the ebbing tide. Wonderful,
elemental in its simplicity. Such power. I
so wish Damian could have been there.**

Gerry Thomas chokes on his cigarette at the
mention of 'Damian'.

                    MIKE

**Have you been there all day? What about
Peony? She was roaming about in her pjs
this morning looking for food.**

SUE nudges her husband.

                    GERRY

Damian bloody Flynn is a charlatan Anna-

Marie. He knows nothing about sculpture. I've told Heidi twenty times that I could get you a proper class with a proper teacher and...

ANNA-MARIE

Not again Gerry please! Peony knows exactly where Hans is camped. Mike, what are you driving at exactly?

SUE

You're wrong Gerry, he's taught us all a lot. Just look at the work Heidi is producing.

GERRY THOMAS stops coughing and tries to get a word in but HELEN COOPER and ROB BECKETT ride up on mountain bikes. She is trim and fit, he is ten years younger, sun bleached blonde and athletic. They both wear skin tight Lycra. HELEN joins the conversation as if she where party to the scene.

HELEN

feisty, out of breath.

Damian Flynn is a wonderful teacher and a lovely man. If it wasn't for him and his class I don't think I would be quite sane.

GERRY

Takes a deep drag and speaks soto-voce as he exhales

You're not all there anyway.

                    HELEN

What did you say?

                    MIKE

You coming tonight Rob?

                 ROB BECKETT

Australian

**You better believe it mate but first I'm off
for a dip.**

BECKETT powers off in low gear. HELEN looks
after him torn between a row with GERRY and
getting BECKETT out of his Lycra. The sex wins
and she rides off after him after glowering at
GERRY.

                  ANNA-MARIE

**Well I must get off, I've a vegetable
casserole to prepare.**

                    MIKE

Hopeful

Oh, aren't you coming to Constantine?

                  ANNA-MARIE

**Of course I'm coming. It was Damian who
suggested the sunsets were spectacular.**

                    MIKE

**Actually as I understand it Charles has
been coming here for years.**

GERRY

Casserole? You're taking a casserole to a barbecue?

ANNA-MARIE

There are more carcinogens produced in barbecued meat than in that disgusting weed you're choking on. I would have thought that as a teacher you'd show more responsibility.

GERRY

Ironic

Yeah you're right and correct me but wasn't it at the last kids party you were passing a joint around?

ANNA-MARIE

Looking to the sky and turns and walks away

That was pure grass, no nicotine, not addictive, doesn't give you cancer.

GERRY

Bloody woman. She you later.

Walks out of scene. MIKE and SUE enter their tent.

3. INT. DAY   THE WILLIAMS' TENT   3.

The interior of the tent is well organised. A kitchen area is tidy and hanging 'cupboards' contain clothing. MIKE sorts out a clean sport's shirt and collects a towel.

MIKE

I'm getting a shower, won't be long

SUE

I hope Gerry isn't going to be sniping at Anna-Marie all night. He is such a pain when he gets a bee in his bonnet.

MIKE

He's right though love, I mean he's a proper teacher and he sells paintings as well. Charles is a serious painter with a following, he sells for serious wedge. It must get up their nose watching her pissing around and talking about elemental simplicity. All we hear from her is Damian said this and Damian showed us that.

SUE

Naughty grin

You might be surprised at what Damian has been showing us

MIKE

Sensing mischief and turning as he was about to leave

What d'you mean you naughty girl? He's gay isn't he?

SUE

Definitely not. His girlfriend is our main model

MIKE

Starting to lose interest

Oh, I didn't know that but you must admit, he's a bit effeminate isn't he.

SUE

Collecting her shower gear

Absolutely not. The opposite in fact. Who do you think posed for the Long Man?

SUE leaves the tent leaving MIKE looking incredulous and smiling.

4. EXT. DAY   CARAVAN/CAMPSITE   OUTSIDE   A
SMALL BATTERED CARAVAN   4.

An equally battered elderly Citroen Safari estate stands nearby. BRIDGET FAIRBROTHER is packing the back of the car. Dressed casually in old denims and a loose fitting tee shirt, everything is calm. CHARLES FAIRBROTHER enters scene. He is a big man, over six feet and eighteen stone he wears a sleeveless, knee length wet suit and his long greying hair is tied in a ponytail. He has a long 'unfashionable' beard and carries snorkel and flippers plus two live lobsters. He is accompanied by his son GILES, equally tall but athletically built and GILES' girlfriend CINDY. CHARLES flops in a camping chair BRIDGET has fetched from an awning as he appeared. She takes the lobsters from CHARLES. She is comfortable with the situation.

BRIDGET

Hot chocolate everybody?

CHARLES

A little out of breath

Thank you darling, boil those little buggers will you please, they'll do for this evening.

GILES and CINDY haven't broken stride towards a nearby tent.

GILES

No chocolate for me thanks mother

CINDY nods enthusiastically to BRIDGET.

GILES Continued

Have you got anything we could eat tonight?

BRIDGET

Don't worry, I've got a couple of steaks for you two, we'll see you there.

CHARLES

Calling after GILES

I enjoyed this afternoon.

GILES doesn't look back but raises a hand in acknowledgement.

CHARLES To BRIDGET

You start to realise you're getting on when your son starts to watch over you.

                    BRIDGET

How d'you mean?

                    CHARLES

Well, the sea was quite choppy today but I wanted to get some lobster or a couple of crabs for tonight and when he saw me heading for the rocks he decided to string along. He didn't say anything or get involved but he hovered and was keeping an eye on me...

He smiles.

   ...seems like yesterday I was teaching the little blighter to dive.

                    BRIDGET

Puts an arm around her husband

How do you feel about that?

                    CHARLES

That's the point. It was great. I felt, I don't know, proud, protected all of that and later as we walked up the beach I was thinking "look everybody, that's my son," I must be getting senile.

                    BRIDGET

There's plenty of life in the old dog yet. I won't have you put down... now, shower, change, we're off shortly.

BRIDGET enters the caravan as HANS MULLER ENTERS SCENE. He is another big man, taller than FAIRBROTHER. He also sports a beard and wears glasses.

                    HANS

German accent

    Hello Charles, a good day?

                    CHARLES

    **Good evening Hans, yes very good. How are
    you?**

                    HANS

    **Good thank you. Tell me, would you have room
    in your car for me this evening? Anna-Marie
    is taking the children but I don't really
    wish to travel as a party and it seems a
    waste to take another car just for me.**

                    CHARLES

    **Of course Hans, you're always welcome. I
    understand Peter wants us to travel in
    convoy so if you could be here in...**

Consults a heavy diving watch.

    ... fifteen minutes or so.

                    HANS

    That is goot, thank you

5. INT. DAY INSIDE A CAMPER VAN   5.
____

HELEN and BECKETT lie post coitus sharing a
joint.

BECKETT

You sure you want to go tonight?

HELEN

Bloody right I do. I'm the only one who supports Anna-Marie. Bloody Gerry Thomas and that pratt Middleton seem to make a point of putting her down. I won't have it. I owe her too much.

BECKETT

Easy babe. She seems perfectly able to take care of herself to me. She ignores them like she ignores everybody else.

HELEN

Getting heated

What d'you mean?

BECKETT

Hands up in surrender

Nothing, nothing. Are we taking any grub?

HELEN

No we'll take some beers and a bit of smoke but Anna-Marie is making a veggy casserole, that'll do us

BECKETT

Pained

Aw babe, I need more than the odd nut burger,

need to keep up the beef bayonet don't I?
Ain't we got no meat?

                    HELEN

With distain

    Please.

Outside a car horn sounds. BECKETT pulls aside
a curtain and opens the window.

6. EXT.DAY.CARAVAN/CAMPSITE BECKETT'S POV 6.

The Discovery is in convoy with the Audi, the
Safari and the Mondeo. Nearby ANNA-MARIE is
loading a 2CV. Her children argue over who holds
a baseball bat. PETER MIDDLETON is halfway out
of the Discovery's window.

                    MIDDLETON

    **Come on you lot. Tuck in behind Gerry. We're
    stopping in Saint Mirren for supplies.**

Mid close up BECKETT.

                    BECKETT

    No rivers mate. We'll catch you later.

Back to mid shot MIDDLETON.

                    MIDDLETON

    **Oh say no more chief. Bit of afternoon
    delight what. Well don't be late, you'll
    miss all the fun.**

Still leaning out of the car window, MIDDLETON does a circular motion with his hand.

                    MIDDLETON

Head 'um up, move 'um out.

MIDDLETON roars away. MIKE WILLIAMS looks to heaven and follows. The convoy leaves scene.

7. EXT. DAY.A VILLAGE CROSS ROADS   7.

The cross roads has shops on three corners and a garage on the fourth. PETER MIDDLETON'S Discovery pulls into the garage. The Audi parks outside the grocery store, the Safari draws up behind the Audi but due to the narrowness of the road there isn't anywhere convenient for GERRY THOMAS' Mondeo.

8. INT. DAY.   THE THOMAS' CAR   8.

                    GERRY

Irritable

Where are we supposed to go? There's nowhere to park.

                    HEIDI

Placating as usual

Pull in behind Peter in the garage. I'll pop out and get the wine, what would you like?

GERRY

Reversing the car

**No, no, sit there. I'll get in behind
Charles.**

HEIDI

There's not enough room.

9. EXT DAY.   CROSS ROADS   9.

As GERRY reverses, a tourist coach arrives
blocking the road. GERRY stops and drives
forward to allow the coach to pass but a car
towing a horse box has filled the space. The
driver of the car with the horse box indicates
that he cannot reverse and the coach has pulled
up close to the Mondeo. THOMAS gesticulates to
the coach driver to reverse but cars have built
up behind the coach. Hooting begins. What was
a backwater is now traffic jam. PETER MIDDLETON
comes out of the garage shop and walks through
the traffic carrying a huge box containing his
new barbecue. MIKE WILLIAMS comes out of the
grocery shop carrying a box of supplies, he
realises that where he has parked is causing
the jam. He puts his supplies on FAIRBROTHER'S
Safari bonnet and starts to direct traffic.
THOMAS is arguing with the coach driver.
MIDDLETON reaches the epicentre.

MIDDLETON

**What d'you think of this Gerry? It's great,
only forty quid.**

GERRY

Beyond incredulous

What!

MIKE

Arriving into scene

Peter you're blocking the garage which is stopping the traffic because the guy with the horse box is trying to get in, If you get moving up there…

MIKE is pointing in all directions as he continues.

… then that lot can go down there and the horse box can pull in where I am, Gerry can pull around the corner, Charles and I can slot in behind Gerry so the coach can get through. You turn around up the road and by the time you get back the traffic will have cleared and you can pass us and lead on. Gerry, you pull up round the corner when Peter's gone….

MIDDLETON

So what do you think? Shall I get it or not?

FAIRBROTHER

From his car

You can just follow us Mike, Peter knows where he's going

                    GERRY

Just get out of the bloody way Peter.

                  MIDDLETON

Still talking about his barbecue

What do you reckon Mike?

                COACH DRIVER

From his cab

   **Just somebody make their bloody mind up
   will yer!**

                    MIKE

Calmly

   Buy the barbecue Peter and move your car.

He starts to direct, talking politely to other
drivers.

   **You move back a little…. You hold it there
   and when he's gone pull in and wait… You and
   you go up that way, then, when I move you
   pull up here, then, once the coach is out
   of the way, you can carry on…**

He turns to the COACH DRIVER who is leaning out
of his window.

   …thank you for your help Sir.

The COACH DRIVER gives a casual 'finger'.
Following instructions the jam begins to
disperse. As the cross road finally clears ANNA-
MARIE drives through in the 2CV. She and the

children wave.

10. EXT. DAY. A COUNTRY LANE IN SIGHT OF THE
SEA   10.

It is early evening. The lane leads down to
the beach and ANNA-MARIE is reversing the 2CV
into the last remaining space in a small car
park. The Safari leads the convoy down the
lane and stops before the car park. Families
are leaving the beach carrying bags and wind
breaks but no cars are being loaded.

11. INT. DAY. EARLY EVENING. F A I R B R O T H E R S
CAR   11.

                    CHARLES

Relaxed

   Looks like there isn't any space.

12. EXT. DAY. EARLY EVENING   FAIRBROTHER'S
POV   12.

Fierce looking elderly woman stands by an open
five bar gate. A badly written notice proclaims
"All day parking £5.00".

                    CHARLES
   **That wasn't there last year, that was just
   a lump of scrub. Well we better get in
   there, nowhere else around.**

CHARLES drives into the entrance and speaks to the woman

                    CHARLES

Good evening, we're just here for the sunset.

                    WOMAN

Stern

We close at eight, it's five pound.

13. EXT.DAY.EARLY EVENING.LANE AND FIELD   13.

Cars in the lane are starting to hoot. FAIRBROTHER drives into the field. WILLIAM and THOMAS follow and park alongside the Safari. The families decar and start to unload. WILLIAMS approaches CHARLES and BRIDGET as HANS gets out of the car. CHARLES looks perplexed.

                    MIKE

What's the problem Charles?

                    CHARLES

Well she wants to shut at eight which means we will have to come back and hope to find somewhere in the main carpark. Sunset's at eight thirty.

They have been walking towards the gate. MIDDLETON drives in much too fast, scattering dust. The elderly woman glares after the Land Rover as MIDDLETON parks next to the other cars. MIKE, CHARLES and BRIDGET reach the gate.

                         WOMAN

Firm

    We close at eight, five pounds per car.

                        BRIDGET

Sweetness and light

    **Is there any chance you could help us?
    We've only come for the sunset, which is so
    beautiful here, you're so lucky, could you
    just give us until nine?**

The WOMAN is starting to melt when MIDDLETON
strides up carrying two cold boxes and his
new, still packaged, barbecue.

                       MIDDLETON

    **What's with old mother Hubbard, this is
    common land isn't it...**

                         WOMAN

    **These gates will be locked at eight, it's
    five pounds per car and there's a fifty pound
    per car overnight charge if you're locked
    in. If you're trying to not pay the five
    pounds now I'll be calling the police after
    I'm locking the gates.**

                         MIKE

    **I'm terribly sorry madam, this gentleman
    didn't mean to be rude and there may have
    been a misunderstanding...**

He produces a twenty pound note from nowhere.

… please take this and if you could give us a little lee way to see the sunset I'd really appreciate it. We'll be back to move the cars straight after eight thirty and there'll be something else for you when we get here. It really is a lovely spot here isn't it?

The WOMAN is mollified by the twenty and MIKE'S ingratiating tone but gives MIDDLETON a dirty look as he shrugs and carries on into the dunes. All the party including children are loaded with cold boxes, wind breaks and baskets of booze. GERRY THOMAS is the last to leave.

CHARLES

As he walks beside MIKE. He laughs.

You use a twenty pound note like a flick knife Mike! It's just a short walk through the dunes then along the beach a bit, we'll find a sheltered spot.

He leads off.

14. EXT. DAY. EARLY EVENING. C O N S T A N T I N E
BEACH EXTREME WIDE SHOT   14.

Most families are packing up and leaving as the group trudge along the beach. Surfers on Malibu boards are catching waves.

15. EXT.DAY.EARLY EVENING.CLOSER ON GROUP 15.

The Thomas and Williams families trudge along together, all fully laden.

                        GERRY

The dunes are bloody miles away.

                         SUE

Never mind Gerry, Charles has been coming
here for years. I'm sure it'll be worth it.

                        MIKE

surveying the sky

We could do with more cloud. If you want
a really good sunset you need a bit of
cloud. It's more dramatic as the sun hits
the clouds from below as it drops over the
horizon.

                        GERRY

I need a bloody drink.

                        HEIDI

Do try to stop complaining Gerry.

                        MIKE

We were shooting in Tunisia a couple of
years ago and wanted a sunset. The cameraman
decided to shoot dawn in reverse to get two
goes at it, you know, shoot dawn in reverse
then at the end of the day shoot the actual
sunset, we only had a couple of days in the
desert. Anyway this local 'fixer' gets us
set up before dawn on top of a dune and as
the sky begins to lighten we all get ready.
The cameraman has his eye to the camera
and we're all staring into what we think

is the east when we feel heat on the back of our necks. We all spin round and the sun is coming up fast behind us. We all go garratty and the bloke say's "as God is my witness it's never done that before".

Mike is laughing but they've all heard the story before.

                    HEIDI

Damian spent time in the desert didn't he Sue?

                    GERRY

Must have suited him that, always said he was a little toe rag.

                    MIKE

Not so little it seems.

                    GERRY

How d'you mean?

                    MIKE

Well, you've seen Sue's 'Long Man', seems our Damian was the model. I'd always assumed she was using her very vivid imagination but she reckons it's from life.

GERRY'S mouth drops open. He looks from SUE to HEIDI who both return his look with challenge.

                    GERRY

Heidi, you've done that one. You mean the bastard's been flashing you as well as

pretending he can teach!

SUE laughs and continues her slog after the children. HEIDI follows her leaving GERRY dumbfounded.

                    HEIDI

Get over it Gerry.

16. EXT. DAY. EARLY EVENING.   THE GROUP BY A BARBED WIRE FENCE   16.

The group has reached the dunes to find a barbed wire fence with a sign to keep people out due to erosion and the planting of Marron Grass to combat the movement of the dune. Everybody dumps their stuff.

                    CHARLES

Oh, that's a shame, we'll set up right here shall we?

                    GERRY

We could of set up a mile back. What a fiasco.

The children drop their burdens and take off like a pack towards the sea. MIDDLETON begins to unpack his new barbecue as FAIRBROTHER sets up a small battered tin box. MIKE breaks out the beers and uncorks a bottle of wine. ANNA-MARIE strolls off towards the shore as the other women set up blankets, chairs and picnic makings. HANS accepts a beer from MIKE and settles down in a chair with Bertram Russell.

HELEN COOPER and BECKETT arrive and GILES FAIRBROTHER and his girlfriend CINDY run up the beach carrying their boards.

GILES

Surf's up Rob, coming in?

BECKETT

Sure thing mate, can I borrow your board Cindy?

BECKETT peels off his jeans and tee shirt and taking the offered board sets off down the beach with GILES. CINDY accepts a glass of Rose and sits on the sand next to HANS.

CINDY

Russell?

HANS

(removing his glasses)

You are familiar?

CINDY

Umm, I'm reading psychology at Portsmouth, we do a bit of philosophy…

HANS

Ah, really, good. This is of course my subject. I'm chair at Leeds.

CINDY's eyes widen. Middleton empties a whole bag of charcoal into his enormous barbecue. FAIRBROTHER already has his going and has settled back with a drink.

MIKE

D'you need a couple of firelighters Peter?

MIDDLETON

No no, thanks anyway Mike. I've got this fluid stuff….

He squirts liberal amounts all over the charcoal.

… you just squirt it straight on and Bob's your aunty.

He puts a lighter to the charcoal and a sheet of flame erupts singeing his eyebrows before dying back immediately. MIKE smiles and turns to FAIRBROTHER whose tin box is glowing nicely with a few sausages on the go.

MIKE

Can I throw some chicken on yours Charles? I'll get mine going later if Peter doesn't achieve lift off.

MIDDLETON

Oh ye of little faith. This is the real McKoy mate.

GERRY

Did you hear the latest about bloody Damian Charles?

CHARLES

No, what was that Gerry?

GERRY

The pratt is only posing for them now.

BRIDGET

They alternate actually Gerry, him and his girlfriend. One poses while the other supervises us.

CHARLES

Makes a kind off sense I suppose. It might account for how well you've all done, the girlfriend must have some talent.

BRIDGET

That's unfair Charles, you've only met him once.

ANNA-MARIE returns to the group and begins to unpack an earthenware pot, French bread and a plastic box of salad from a large wicker basket. The others watch fascinated for a while. MIDDLETON'S barbecue erupts in another sheet of flames.

ROSEMARY

I think you're all being unfair to Damian. His art class has been a tremendous help to me. He started the class. He's an inspiration, what do you say Sue?

SUE

I agree with you entirely Rosemary. I have the pressure of a career as well as a family like you and being married to Mike is stressful enough believe me….

She smiles to show she is being good humoured and Mike grins and shrugs.

…. We're either filthy rich or totally broke and I find the sculpture class not only fulfilling but almost like yoga, meditation. It helps me relax.

CHARLES

(turning sausages and chicken legs)

I understand what you're saying Sue but if it's so relaxing and the class is fulfilling and don't get me wrong, I'm not knocking what you've said but why are your pieces all so inward? Every one I've seen has been a woman crouching, huddled, back hunched against the world. It all looks stressed to me.

MIKE

(pouring wine and handing out tins of beer)

You obviously haven't seen the 'Long Man' then Charles.

MIDDLETON

(trying to coax life into his charcoal)

What d'you mean 'The Long Man?'

ANNA-MARIE

(exasperated, resigned)

We did a male study some months back Peter, for which Damian posed. We all worked very hard and Sue produced a beautiful abstract in which she elongated the entire physique. We all agreed it was her best work and that she captured a true representation of our guru; she called it 'The long Man.'

MIDDLETON

leaving the charcoal

Oh, like your one Rosemary. I thought you were using your imagination, bit of wishful thinking. Are you telling me that was a 'true representation.'

GERRY

Must be built like a bull Rhinoceros if Heidi's is anything to go by.

GILES and BECKETT return from the surf and stand dripping in brief swimming trunks and everybody finds themselves watching as they towel themselves.

BECKETT

What's up?

ANNA-MARIE

Why is it all men seem to have a penis fixation? They are either dis-proportionately proud and believe the size of their dong is worth bringing into every conversation or they're convinced it's too small and tell everybody 'size doesn't matter.'

HELEN

What do you say Hans?

HANS

removing his glasses again

Anna-Marie of course has a point, however I believe she, as always, generalises too much. There are men who behave as she describes but I do not believe 'all' men are or think so.

There is of course another aspect to the sculpture under discussion. Maybe the ladies of the class have over emphasised the overt maleness in their teacher, or guru as Anna-Marie quaintly describes him, to compensate for or to disagree with the reactions of their partners to the man Damian. By showing him to be so substantial in that particular part of his anatomy they reject the beliefs of their husbands that he is less than substantial as a teacher, or as a man. It is interesting is it not that they acclaim Sue's work which, if I am correct, emphasises the elongated penis particularly.

The whole group pause, each considering their response, then several speak at once.

                    MIDDLETON

referring to his barbecue

    I'm sure it's going now.

                    CHARLES

holding up a sausage on a fork

    Sauso anyone?

                    GERRY

lighting a 'roll-up'

    You're probably right Hans

                    ANNA-MARIE

    The man's in a world of his own

                    SUE

    Well, it is in the abstract

                    MIKE

    I'll drink to that.

                    ROSEMARY

    Peter, why isn't our food ready?

                    HELEN

grabbing BECKETT'S arm and leading him towards
the fence and the dunes

    Come on Rob, I want to talk to you..

                    MIKE

grinning

   You two will miss the sunset

The children have returned dripping and the
mothers distribute towels, burgers and sausages.
MIDDLETONS barbecue is loaded with raw meat, a
thin trail of smoke is all that signifies heat
or life. GERRY THOMAS sets up his barbecue.

                    GERRY

   **We'll be all night waiting for you Peter,
   why won't you use a firelighter?**

                  MIDDLETON

getting uptight

   **This fluid is fine, you don't need firelighters
   these days.**

MIKE is distributing food from FAIRBROTHERS
tin box. Fairbrother adds his lobsters.

                    MIKE

   **There's plenty of life left in this Gerry,
   why don't you use it when Charles has done
   his lobster?**

GERRY mutters as he drags on his roll-up.

                    HEIDI

   **No Mike, he's got to get his going so he can
   find something else to moan about now we've
   established that if Damian didn't exist we
   would probably create him. Meanwhile we**

don't eat.

                    GERRY

irritable, puzzled

What?

                    ROSEMARY

I'd offer you some of ours to be getting on with Heidi but I'm not sure I fancy it much myself.

                    MIDDLETON

stroppy

If you'd just be patient, barbecued food should be cooked slowly.

He turns the burgers and chops. The sides now exposed are black, the other sides are raw.

ANNA-MARIE ladles out bowls of vegetable casserole. Her children tuck in but the boy has been slipped a burger by MIKE and is keeping it hidden.

                    ANNA-MARIE

It's going to be a beautiful sunset

                    MIKE

a little tipsy

I don't know, we could do with more cloud. You must have cloud for a proper sunset...

MIDDLETON carefully takes the grill off his

barbecue and squirts more liquid. Another sheet of flame erupts and he quickly puts the grill back dropping some burgers into the sand as he does.

ROSEMARY

Peter, please use Charles', the children are hungry…

MIDDLETON

back turned, hunched over the barbecue

Patience please, it's going well now.

ROSEMARY

Oh, for Christ's sake, he drives me bonkers.

SUE

Have a piece of chicken Rosemary, the kids are alright they've had a burger.

MIKE

Have another glass of wine Rosemary.

GERRY is quietly grilling fish. He is sprinkling herbs and seems happy – for a change.

HEIDI to ROSEMARY

It's one of the few times he stops grumbling, cooking or painting. I sometimes think they've a similarity. They're both creative aren't they?

SUE

I think you're right Heidi. I've never really 'enjoyed' cooking but since I started with the class I'm getting more out of the kitchen…. Does Peter normally cook Rosemary?

ROSEMARY

You must be joking. And he's not actually cooking now is he.

General laughter.

MIDDLETON

trying to stay calm

I heard that. Teething trouble, that's all.

BRIDGET

eating lobster from the shell

I do the day to day stuff but Charles does all the exotic work. I think you're right too Heidi, I know several artists who are great cooks.

SUE

Mike likes to cook but he's away so often.

ROSEMARY

Do you ever go with him on location Sue?

SUE

Not really, it's actually really boring being on set if you're not part of the

team or actively involved and when it's advertising he's always on parade. That lot expect to be entertained every night and they're all like spoilt children...

BRIDGET

You were away with him last year wasn't you?

SUE

Oh yes that was great. A lot of the film was shot in and around Sydney and the atmosphere on a movie is totally different, it was lovely, I got this there.

SUE WILLIAMS has been wearing a striking Ken Done tee shirt all evening and has covered up with an Aran jumper as the evening drew in. She pulls up the jumper to show the tee shirt but gets hold of the tee shirt as well and as she lifts her arms and draws the jumper over her head. The group is treated to a grand view of her bare breasts. MIKE collapses with laughter, CHARLES grins, the other women shriek, as does SUE as she hastily covers up and red-faced tries to explain that she meant to show the tee shirt. PETER and GERRY were too engrossed with their barbecues to have seen the show and GERRY reacts with bemusement.

GERRY

What?

MIDDLETON

not turning around

Yes, yes, we're away, we're cooking

17. EXT. EVENING.   WIDE SHOT OF GROUP FOCUS TWARDS THE SEA AND THE SUNSET   17.

As the group settles down after the laughter, GILES and CINDY take up their boards and run off to catch THE SUNSET WAVES. The huge red orb dominates the horizon. Everybody is silent. Even the children stand mesmerised as colour streaks across the sea and sky. HELEN and BECKETT return from the dunes and sit quietly. HELEN takes her stash from a backpack and begins to construct a three paper joint. BECKETT accepts a beer from MIKE and also sits staring at the sun.

18. EXT. EVENING.MID SHOT GROUP   18.

MIKE

More wine anybody?

At the 'Magic Moment' through the group, camera zooms to find GILES catching a wave and travelling fifty or sixty yards with the setting sun throwing him into sharp silhouette before he sinks gracefully into the spent surf. He collects his board and strides up the beach towards the group. Cindy joins him, still both in silhouette.

CHARLES

off camera

Yeah!

ROSEMARY

off camera

God, I wish I could do that.

GERRY

off camera

You ought to get young Giles to pose for you.

SUE

off camera

Don't you think we've thought of that.

MIKE

off camera good natured

Behave you lot!

<u>19. EXT. LATE EVENING.   BACK   TO   WIDE   OF</u>
<u>GROUP   19.</u>

PETER MIDDLETON squirts lighter fluid resulting in another sheet of flame.

MIDDLETON

as a football chant

'ere we go, 'ere we go, 'ere we go

The sun sinks below the horizon leaving the group lit only by the twilight and the sheets of flame erupting as MIDDLETON sends more and more fluid into the conflagration which was to have been his family's supper. One by one the party begin to pack up and trudge off in family groups. MIDDLETON is left in the darkness manically squirting fluid and turning the burnt offerings.

<u>20. LATE EVENING. TRACKING SHOT FURTHER ALONG THE BEACH</u>   20.

Cut between various groups.

                    HEIDI

arm in arm with her husband

>**The fish was delicious darling.**

                    GERRY

mellow

>**Hmm**

                    BRIDGET

arm in arm with Charles

>**You don't really mind Damian posing for us do you?**

                    CHARLES

smiling warmly

>**What do you think?**

                    GILES

walking with CINDY, HELEN and BECKETT

**Shall we try the 'Head' tonight or d'you
fancy going into Newquay?**

HELEN

holding onto BECKETT

There's a party at the Bay Hotel…

BECKETT

looking at HELEN with a manic expression

The Head sounds good to me…

HELEN elbows him in the ribs.

SUE

arm in arm with MIKE

I think I better drive.

MIKE

looking at his watch

Shit! The car park!

21. EXT. NIGHT.IN THE LANE OUTSIDE THE FIVE
BAR GATE.   21.

The scene is lit by a single public lamp post.
The gate is padlocked.

GERRY

back in character

Bloody   marvellous,   bloody   bleeding

marvellous.

                    ROSEMARY

to ANNA-MARIE who is heading for the official
carpark

   **Could you take Penelope please Anna-Marie,
   she's very tired.**

                   ANNA-MARIE

   **Looks like I will have to take everybody.
   I'll run a shuttle service.**

                     HELEN

   **We can take Rosemary and the kids. We'll
   sort them out when we get back to the site.
   Rob parked the camper just up the road.**

                      SUE

   **Well the Cornish Arms is near, we'll make our
   way there and if you wouldn't mind coming
   back for us Rob we'd really appreciate it.
   What about Peter, Rosemary?**

                    ROSEMARY

   Oh fuck Peter *and* his fucking barbecue.

<u>21. NIGHT.MID SHOT PETER MIDDLETON IN THE
DARK   21.</u>

The barbecue has died, MIDDLETON stands holding
the lighter fluid bottle in one hand and a
spatula in the other. In the dark we can just
make out his expression of bemusement.

   END.

Train Ride To Death
- Maggie Taylor

He picked her out as soon as she walked down the platform of the city railway station. She was in her sixties judging by her white hair but smartly dressed in what looked to be expensive clothes. She was wearing sunglasses and carrying a large tote bag, both 'designer' he thought.

She was slim, average in height and in spite of a slight limp she carried herself well. He followed her into a carriage of the waiting train and sat down opposite to her.

It was 'senior's card time' after 9.30am so the train wasn't very full and most of the other passengers were elderly too. He pretended to be looking at the screen of his mobile phone but in reality he was watching her. She was wearing an expensive looking gold watch and had several gold chains around her neck. Her wedding ring and diamond engagement ring on her left hand were matched by two other large rings on her right hand.

Then an elderly man sat down beside her and they started to talk to each other. He had never understood why older people seemed to need to talk to each other and decided it was a generational thing. They were discussing the article on the front page of the newspaper the man was carrying.

"He seems very hard to catch," said the woman.

"Well the police are underfunded and undermanned," replied the man, "so it's not surprising that these people get away with so much these days."

"But he always strikes in broad daylight and no-one ever

seems to see him. It's only when they find the body that they know a crime has been committed."

"That's because life is more dangerous these days than when I was young," replied the man. "I fought in two world wars and I didn't feel as insecure then as I do now. I hesitate to go out of my house sometimes."

"Oh dear, that's a shame," said the woman shaking her head. "We should be able to walk down the street safely. I can remember when we didn't even lock our doors or our cars at night and that's not so long ago."

The train slowed down for the next station and the man stood up. "Nice talking to you," he said, "but this is my stop so I'll say goodbye.

"Goodbye!" said the woman. "Stay safe."

He was pleased that the man had got off, altogether too chummy he thought. It could have been a problem.

But now the woman was collecting her things and standing up ready to get off at the next station. He followed her off the train but kept well back and blended in with the other passengers on the platform.

It was quite an 'upmarket' area and he hoped she didn't have someone meeting her, but she kept walking out of the station and along a nearby street. For her age she was a surprisingly fast walker. They were approaching a café strip and he thought she was going to stop but she had just slowed down to look in a shop window before she turned left into a quiet residential street.

About halfway down she turned into the driveway of a well maintained, federation style house. Although quite old these houses had soared in value over the recent years and the suburb was one of old money and conservative traditions, mostly populated by the elderly who had bought their houses many years before. Although most of the houses had been renovated and updated they had kept their original facades.

It was getting better and better as far as he was concerned because these houses all had a laneway behind them. It was designed initially for the 'night soil' cart but now it provided access to their back gardens.

He waited until she had unlocked the front door and gone inside, then he walked past and kept going until he reached the next cross street where he turned left. Sure enough there was a laneway and he sauntered along it until he was behind the woman's house. He knew it was the right house because he had studied the colour and shape of the roof but it had a high wall and a secured gate opening on to the laneway. Fortunately the house next door only had a wire mesh fence and an easily opened gate.

He paused a while but no-one stirred and no dogs barked so he went into the garden. The dividing fence was an asbestos one and the supporting wooden framework was on his side so it was easy to climb up and look over it. There were plenty of mature shrubs and trees on the other side to give him cover so he rapidly climbed over the fence and dropped down into her garden.

Again he waited but there was no sign of life so using the cover of the shrubs he made his way slowly along the fence towards the house. The garden was terraced and the area closest to the house was an open lawned area with some garden chairs and a table. Again he traversed it quickly and no-one seemed to have seen him.

Now he was up close to the house and he saw a glass French window which allowed access to the garden. He edged along towards it and to his surprise it wasn't locked. Cautiously he peered into the room. It was furnished as a dining room with a long table and eight chairs and a sideboard along the wall. No one was visible so hardly believing his luck he went inside.

At one end of the room was a kitchen and the other end opened out into a large sitting room. Both rooms were deserted so he walked into a passageway which opened off the dining room. There were several doors each side of it, presumably bedrooms and bathrooms he thought. Still moving silently he crept along it and opened doors slightly as he passed but there was no sign of the elderly woman. Until he came to the end of the passage and there was one door left. It was half open and there she was, lying on a bed with her eyes closed. Her shoes lay on the floor where she had kicked them off.

He could almost feel his hands around her throat and see her death struggles as she fought for breath. He moved towards the bed and reached over to make it reality, when she suddenly shot upright and grabbed him around his neck in a strong grip and twisted his body down onto the side of the bed. At the same time footsteps raced down the hall and the elderly man rushed into the room, pinioned his arms behind him and slapped on handcuffs.

"Got you, you bastard," said the elderly woman who was looking a lot less elderly now her wig had fallen off in the struggle exposing blond hair. The elderly man had also undergone surprising rejuvenation as he stood over the man on the floor.

"WPC Helen Drummond," said the woman, "and I am arresting you for attempted murder and I am sure we will find your

DNA matches what we found at the site of four other murders of elderly women who have been murdered and robbed in the last six months.

"Detective Sergeant Adrian Murray," said the 'elderly' man. "You should have varied your M.O. Charlie. It was only a matter of time before we made the connection that all your victims had been riding on a train shortly before they were killed in their houses, though it was interesting watching you creep up to the house."

"But you got off the train," stuttered Charlie.

"No, that was just an illusion Charlie. I got back on again in another carriage, so I was following you, following her. Piece of cake really. Now on your feet, there's a Police car waiting in the drive to take you to the next phase of your life; incarceration. Let's go and well done Helen! You'll make a very spunky old lady when you get there."

About the authors......

Teena Raffa-Mulligan

Teena Raffa-Mulligan is a reader, writer and daydream believer who is convinced there is magic in every day if you choose to find it. Teena discovered the wonderful world of stories as a child and knew she wanted to be a writer from an early age. She writes quirky, whimsical books for children and fun, flirty romances. Her writing life has also included a long career in journalism. Teena shares her passion for books and writing by presenting talks and workshops to encourage people of all ages to write their own stories.

Visit her website   www.teenaraffamulligan.com
for more information about her books and writing sessions.

Johanna Baker-Dowdell

A writer from a young age, Johanna has always loved to get to the heart of a person by asking probing questions and sharing their story.

She has worked as a journalist at daily, bi-weekly, weekly and monthly newspapers in Australia and the UK writing news and feature articles on a multitude of topics, including business, agriculture, property and the arts.

Johanna took her career freelance for more than a decade, under her business Strawberry Communications. During this time she wrote the women's business bible 'Business & Baby on Board' and started writing fiction, publishing short stories and memoir pieces in 'Love Alters: A Love for All Seasons' and 'Unfinished Chapters.'

Always looking for ways to develop her experience and knowledge, Johanna studied journalism at the University of Newcastle in New South Wales, following this up with an Honours degree in Journalism, Media and Communication from the University of Tasmania. She is also studying a PhD in journalism with the University of Tasmania, investigating how social media texts are used by newspapers as news sources in reporting crisis events.

Johanna lives with her husband, two sons, a dog, cat and two guinea pigs in Launceston, Tasmania, a beautifully natural space that provides a constant source of inspiration.

Find out more about Johanna's work at johannabd.com

Kelly Van Nelson

Born in the North East of England, Kelly has lived in London, Edinburgh, and Cape Town before immigrating to Australia with her family. She is a mother of two amazing children, and wife to her soul mate of over two decades, Managing Director of a Fortune 500, and bestselling author represented by Clive Newman at The Newman Agency. Kelly is also an advocate for bullying and domestic violence prevention initiatives and founder of the Facebook group, Words Worth, challenging the world through the written, spoken, and visual word. "In short, I'm a Juggler. Now and then, like all jugglers, I drop the ball. That's part of the fun. I like to embrace the unknown, think positively, and live life to its fullest."

In 2019 Kelly was the winner of the AusMumpreneur Big Idea (Changing The World) Award for her literary work in using the spoken, written and visual word to raise awareness on social issues. AusMumpreneur is Australia's #1 community for mum's in business.

Find out more about Kelly at www.kellyvannelson.com

Ross Cameron

Ross worked in advertising and the film business for more than forty years, starting as a runner and becoming a successful producer and managing director. He worked all around the world; had some hair-raising adventures, met some wonderful people (and a lot not so wonderful) and is proud of his fifty years of marriage; a rare record in that particular circus.

He made hundreds of commercials and a feature film set in Chicago with Roger Daltrey. He produced the videos 'China Girl' and 'Let's Dance' with David Bowie in Australia, which went on to win the Grammy for 'Best Video'. His 'fifteen minutes of fame' was probably when Iggy Pop accepted the award in Los Angeles and read out a tribute to his contribution from Bowie (who Ross puts firmly in the wonderful category).

Ross 'officially' retired in 2010, but went on to be a founding director of The Lemon Tree Book Company Ltd with Tracey Regan, writing and publishing children's personalised books. He is now focusing on his memoirs, which will feature some fun and crazy stories about his life in the film industry.

Maggie Taylor

Re-educating herself in her late fifties, Maggie is a qualified naturopath and kinesiologist. She's had a varied and well-travelled life, born in England and moving to Australia….a long time ago (!), raising her two boys 'in the bush', in the hills just outside Perth, WA. She's had a passion for writing for many years and is currently working on her memoirs so her grandchildren will be able to discover all her favourite memories from her life.

Tracey Regan

Tracey describes herself as a 'jack of all trades'. For her writing she draws on life experiences working in a vast variety of professions, and her love of travel. Tracey has worked in the film industry, for a women's weekly magazine, as a lock-keeper at the famous St. Katherine's Dock in London, an outdoor activity instructor in Wales and a sailing instructor in the south of France; an 'apricot cutter' and barmaid in remote Australia (fun stories around those jobs!), and even as a waitress in a Hare Krishna restaurant. She's had a selection of more conventional jobs too, but for the last few years, has been writing and publishing children's personalised books at The Lemon Tree Book Company Ltd. She has a 19 year old daughter, who she is extremely proud of, who is making her on way in the world, working overseas.

Tracey now assists start-ups, businesses and budding writers with 'All Things Writing!'
You can find out more at   www.tregan.biz

SIXTH SENSE

Metallic taste after wind knocked from my sails by
cowards punch

Nostrils flare, parachutes desperately seeking the
pungent scent of air

Sound of foreboding sirens in the distance

Tremble at the sight of pristine white walls closing in

Thankful at the touch of your gentle palm in mine

All five senses heighten as the light beckons

Didn't believe a sixth sense existed until stumbling over
the twisted truth

I sense this is the end.

Kelly Van Nelson